HURDY GURDY

Christopher Wilson's novels include *Gallimauf's Gospel*, *Baa*, *Blueglass*, *Mischief*, *Fou*, *The Wurd*, *The Ballad of Lee Cotton*, *Nookie* and *The Zoo*, which was shortlisted for the HWA Gold Crown Award in 2018. His work has been translated into several languages, adapted for the stage and twice shortlisted for the Whitbread Fiction Prize. Wilson completed a published PhD on the psychology of humour at LSE, worked as a research psychologist at UCL, the London Hospital and the Arts Council, and lectured for ten years at Goldsmiths College, University of London. He has taught creative writing in prisons, at university and for the Arvon Foundation.

Further praise for *Hurdy Gurdy*:

'Wilson's doodles and detours combine into a high-spirited, richly coloured panorama of High Gothic imagery and ideas . . . If our bumptious young healer-monk grabs the last word, Wilson himself has the last laugh. Even in pandemic times, he hints, comedy is the superpower to purge one-eyed, self-deluding humankind.' *Financial Times*

'The core of *Hurdy Gurdy* is the human striving for understanding, be it spiritual or medical, and our capacity for self-delusion.' *Her*

D1340982

'Of the Covid-inflected novels expected this year, few will be as weirdly entertaining as this cautionary tale.' *Mail on Sunday*

'A picaresque road trip . . . The effect is a little like Chaucer as told by Adrian Mole.' *The Spectator*

'A supremely witty, sharp and rollicking piece of satirical storytelling. With echoes of *Candide* and *Don Quixote*, this gem of a novel, following the fate of the hapless novice, Brother Diggory, in his journey of discovery during the Black Death, had me captivated. Laugh-out-loud funny, *Hurdy Gurdy* confirms Christopher Wilson as a truly original voice in historical fiction.' Elizabeth Fremantle

'Gloriously entertaining and profoundly moving . . . Chris is a master of the tragicomic, and one of our finest observers of humanity's definitive absurdities and graces.' Stephen Kelman

'Pleasure in its rawest form.' Bookmunch

---

by the same author

GALLIMAUF'S GOSPEL
BAA
BLUEGLASS
MISCHIEF
FOU
THE WURD
NOOKIE
THE BALLAD OF LEE COTTON
THE ZOO

Christopher Wilson

HURDY GURDY

faber

First published in 2021
by Faber & Faber Limited
Bloomsbury House
74–77 Great Russell Street
London WC1B 3DA

This paperback edition first published in 2021

Typeset by Faber & Faber Limited
Printed and bound by CPI Group (UK) Ltd, Croydon CR0 4YY

A CIP record for this book
is available from the British Library

This is a work of fiction. All of the characters, organisations and
events portrayed in this novel are either products of the author's
imagination or are used fictitiously

ISBN 978–0–571–36195–3

4 6 8 10 9 7 5

For Janet Hesketh
and for Robin Miller Kennedy

I am out with lanterns, looking for myself.
EMILY DICKINSON

ANNO DOMINI
1349–1352

I. The Discovery of Women

When I died the first time, the Good Lord took pity on my boy's frail sparrow frame, caught the fleeing beat of my heart, and blew the breath back into my still-warm body. Then he laid me back into this nest of life, like some tumbled, trampled hatchling, shivering, squawking and ruffle-feathered, judging my death was come too soon, that I still had use, and had to live, learn and suffer more.

This was in the season of the plague, in the twenty-first year of Our Lord King Edward, Long-Hair, the Great Unbuttoned – may God preserve him – who loves his peoples sorely, especially the women.

The world was younger then, still raw. The edges of our Earth had not been mapped, and many oceans and continents remained unknown to folk. The colours were sharp, freshly daubed by His Divine brush, and the sounds new as dew, and the feel of things prickled sharp as nettles. And, yes, I pledge on the jeopardy of my immortal soul. I saw it all, with my young eyes. From start to end.

And may Lucifer, and his infernal demons, make a feet-ball of my bonce, a wine-gourd of my bladder, a purse of my scrotum, then pluck my eye-balls for ink-wells, stretch my guts for bow-strings, fry my liver for break-fast, and griddle my guts for all time, if a word of this sorry history turns out to be a lie.

Never forget. In Hell a man weeps more tears than all the waters of all the oceans. While his brains are boiled in vinegar for all eternity. As his flesh is chewed from his bones by demons. Then straightaway sprouts back to be chewed anew.

But get to know me, first. Here, grasp the sturdy peg of my name, to hang the tale on. To tell me apart from the rest of the stubborn, bleating, woolly, dag-arsed flock. So I am not just another bag of offal and shit, skittering on the hoof, braying his way unthinking to the butcher's hook.

Perhaps you've heard of me before. I'm known as Jack Fox. So I rhyme, face and arse, with the Black Pox.

I was delivered to God's Earth sixteen years before, out of the belly of a woman, clothed in transient flesh, destined for dust, but possessed of an immortal soul.

I became a novice of the Order of Odo. You are given a fresh name when you enter the monastery, for then you are reborn to Christ. So I was baptised Brother Diggory, in my life as a monk.

See it. In your mind's eye. We are *here*, surrounded by the patchwork of pastures and dark woods. In the heart of our soggy, green island, as far from the sea as you can be.

This is our monastery. My home. Before you. God's house at Whye. A long, low, crumbling, grey-stone, thatched hovel, looming out of the mist, like a beasts' barn, slumped next to a ruin, floating in a marsh.

Mind the puddles and cowpats as you trudge close, through the fog of your imagination. Follow the good

4

guidance of your nostrils, and trot dainty around the shit-pit.

The flies are God's ornaments, ignorant and pitiful creatures, like ourselves. They are our moral guides. They remind us even small lives matter. They warn us we are tiny beings, and frail like them, and that some giant hand, or some Divine cow's tail, may suddenly swish down from above, and slap us flat.

Splat.

To a still, damp smudge.

Praise the Lord for the wonders of Creation.

Some creatures He made to soar through the airs, some to trot the earth on cloven hooves, some to squirm the muds like worms, some to swim the depths. Some He made to chew on grass, some to sup on stale shit.

Yet for others He made a plentiful provision of sturgeon simmered in butter with thyme and wild garlic, stuffed with samphire, crayfish tails and chestnuts, crusted with grated cheese, dusted with crocus pollen, to be eaten with golden spoons from crystal bowls in marbled halls. For to each of us He gave a branch to perch, high or low, in the Tree of His Creation.

Smile. It's not so dismal as it first appears. Duck your sorry sinner's head, and stoop to enter in. Your eyes will soon adjust to the gloom. You'll grow used to the odours, too. They arise from the innocent juices of holy men, squirting out from our moist, too-human bodies. On a cold day, at prayer in the chapel, the damp rises from our hunched shoulders like morning mist off the turf. We

5

struggle to keep our hearts clean. But we are leaky sacks of sweaty skin, and we bathe just once a year on Bathday Thursday – just after Lent.

Never care. We wash our feet weekly, on Fridays, for they constantly tread upon the dirt of the world. So any less often would be unclean.

Our founder, Saint Odo of Whye, was a holy spirit in a mighty man, set apart from his fellows, and high above us, through his sanctity, his kindness, and his perfect, flawless ugliness – possessed of a face that left none unmoved. But made bold men wince, gulp and gasp, for they did not recognise the topmost part of him – poking out from his collar – as a human head. For it better suggested some raw lump of gristle. You'd best imagine a throbbing, blood-wet, glistening lump of carcass, discarded on the killing-floor, after a beast was butchered.

Saint Odo the Ugly had two supernatural skills. He had prescience and he had duality.

He could see far ahead. In time. For his herbs – hemlock, poppy, henbane, hemp – advised him. They opened his eyes, to peer through the fogs of nowadays and mists of tomorrows, clear to far future ages.

This way, he saw strange machines, buildings big as mountains, underwater boats, giant metal birds that held people in their bowels, and spewed them out at the front, and shat them out through their back passage, and pestilences, and foul wars to come, and the orange-faced king, Small Hands, with straw-yellow hair wound round his head like a helmet, who said that truths were lies, and lies were truths, that the Seven Acts of Mercy were sins, so the sick should be left to cure themselves, and the homeless should house themselves, the dead should bury themselves, and that the poor should build a wall to keep themselves out.

Also, Odo could bilocate.

That's our Latin scribe's way of saying he could be in two places at once. Or, to tell it another way, appear as two separate people. Albeit identical. And this is why he is known, by his full name, as Saint Odo and Saint Odo, of Here and There.

It's said that Odo could often be found sleeping in his cot in his cell, while nursing the sick in the sanatorium. Or bathing in the lake, while studying in the library. Or chanting in the chapel, while baking bread in the out-house. The variations were endless. And he was known never to spare this great gift, but to always tire it to exhaustion with perpetual, ingenious use.

Now, one hundred and thirty years after his ascent to the heavens, only his skull-bone remains to us, separated from its lower jaw, as a precious relic. It is held in two sealed reliquary chests behind the altar in the chapel. Once a year, on Saint Odo's Day, the Abbot opens the boxes and declares where the bone has found its rest – be it to the left ivory box or the right cedar-wood box.

Then, as always, when it is to be found in both boxes at once, the brothers sing their praises, *O dulcis electe*, with whoops of wonder, and a loud acclaim, knowing it is a certain and remarkable proof that Saint Odo is close, lives on in his noble spirit, and moves amongst us still, both here and there.

Saint Odo left us one marvellous memento. The great gift of his example. For he gave his life to the care of the sick. He tended those wretched and despised. But it's known he reserved his deepest love for the sickest and ugliest, and those most desperately deformed, and the demented, the deluded, the tangle-limbed, the incontinent, the scabby and foul-smelling.

In tending the sick – folk tormented with swellings, boils, scrofula, weeping wounds and sores – he would forever suffer the same contagions of skin himself. Over time, this taxed his complexion, laying scab upon scar, till he gained a patina so bloated, monstrous-scaled, reddened and purpled that he could not show himself to strangers without causing them distress or offence. Or perhaps to drop into a faint. This way he became known as Saint Odo the Disfigured and became patron of the ugly, all those who suffer some blemish of the body or soul, and champion of curs, waifs, dogs and the despised.

Our brotherhood is not a large one like those Benedictines or Carthusians, but a small, poor band of thirty-nine brothers, possessed of a single monastery.

We are known as the Dingy Brothers. For we all wear a cloth of dirty grey. Turned damp brown or black at the hems. We live simply but we do not seek out our poverty like the Franciscans or embrace it like the Dominicans. No. We are poor without trying. We are poor because we are poor. For we have not been blessed with riches.

Not yet. But our time may come, if the Lord only wills it. And we are gentle souls, not fighters like the Hospitallers, Templars or Teutonic Knights.

We strive to live gently, quietly and kindly, like our founder Odo, praising the Lord, praying for the world, studying diseases that we may conquer them, devising medicines, treating the sick, tending our garden, and copying our manuscripts.

Odo's greatest work, his opus magnum was his grand treatise titled *The Book of Life: All that Lives and Breathes in God's Kingdom*, detailing all forms and varieties of life that wander the land, swim the waters and fly the airs, stoke the fires of Hell, and sanctify the heavens. There is not one type of living creature that is not described in his book. This is why it extends over two hundred pages.

Odo also studied anatomy, detailing the organs of the human body, not just of Man but reaching out to Woman too. And so he is credited with the first true discovery of Woman, for he showed beyond contradiction that there was more to woman than met the eye. So that she was not just a small lumpen man with male private parts turned inside out – an invert, as scholars supposed – but a separate and complete form of being, possessed of her very own intricate anatomy, with much more concealed in her deep interior than the outsides ever betrayed.

But, since the dissection of the dead is strictly forbidden by the Church, as a desecration of God's Own handiwork, he derived these careful and exact anatomical truths, concerning Man and Woman, from observing the insides of pigs, which animals, it is to be believed, most closely resemble the human pattern. Providing you disregard the oink, trotters and curly tail. *Mutatis mutandis.*

Praise be to God.

Odo writes too of the Monstrous Tribes of the West, including the Dog-Heads, the Fire-Breathers, the Mermen (half-fish, half-men) and the Giant One-Legs, who cause the ground to shudder as they hop from place to place. The Headless Men are known as Akephaloi or Blemmyes, first discovered by Gervase of Tilbury who came upon them on the Island of Brisone, close by the Two Sicilies. They lack a head or neck. So their face is displaced upon their chest, with the eyes placed where the nipples should be, above a nose in the centre of their chest, with a greedy mouth below, curved to the shape of a horse-shoe.

Their brain is so squashed in their chest by the other organs – lungs, heart and liver – that it makes them giddy and forgetful. So you must not expect much of their wit, science or scholarship. Although they prove jolly and friendly companions, if over-fond of wines.

And Odo also wrote a second, later book, his opus-cule – *The Great Unhappened: Being a Record of the Yet Undone* – which records those things still to come, in a future that only he had seen. Telling of strange objects and events, on their way, coming to future times.

He said there would be viewing-machines which were metal tubes with polished glass ends. Through one end you could see the distant made large. And through the other you could spy the close made small. Depending upon your choice. Also he told of the voice tablets, which were small tiles with a mosaic surface, little enough to lie in the flat of your hand. Yet, if you knew the codex, and touched the exact squares in a certain special sequence, you could speak to people who were not there, but were far away, though they sounded as close as if whispering into your ear. So though they spoke loud, their voices were disembodied. Also, there would be icy cold drinks, in small, squat suits of armour, bursting with bubbles that prickled your tongue. And a metal box with a glass window that cooked your food without any fire, just by turning it through circles on a glass platter. And winter-machines that turned warm, summer waters into ice, flying carriages and music plates, and picture-chests showing the shadows of people, flickering before your eyes as if alive. These are marvellous things to come. Along with monstrous wars and terrible pestilences, as we trudge to the future, alongside Lucifer, strutting, swaggering, aiming to undo us and nudge us into the damp, muddy ditch of sin.

Spare my quills.

This vellum is bristly as Brother Michael's arse.

We brothers live to do God's work. We welcome the wretched and infirm. We take in the destitute and the despised. We maintain a sick-house for the treatment of all ailments, of the body, the mind and the spirit.

Our sacred rules forbid us to laugh. For, as the Abbot always cautions us, we are not beasts, like braying asses, that have lost control of their faculties. Nor bleating sheep, incontinent of our emotions.

11

But we are free to smile on feast days, to show our joy at God's bounty.

And, on the first four Thursdays after Lent, we are welcome to play. Within reason, in moderation. Between Vespers and Compline. But without dice or idolatry. And without any thought of woman.

And here lies my problem.

For, in recent months, I find my thoughts, like wanton, frisky goats, stray from the pastures of my work – my daily tasks of copying and prayer – and jump the fence of discipline, verging upon women.

For women just come to mind. Quite uninvited. By day and by night. And mostly by night. Without welcome, rhyme or reason. There is no respite from their visitations. Not even while I sleep. For I have even begun to dream of them. Of She. Of Her.

The Nameless One.

Who comes to me in my deepest slumber so I wake startled, my swollen loins inflamed, with a fear and a shame and a throbbing ache. But She is just some spirit of the dark, who is gone as soon as I wake and flick open my startled eyes.

II. Succubus

I know enough. There is evil here, and sin clinging close. And danger in its shadows. So I ask Brother Fulco for a special confession.

He is the master, and I am the pupil.

He was appointed my mentor, to cuff my ears and guide my eternal soul. He has raised me with piety, and a kindness well hidden behind a harsh tongue and a hard hand. He taught me the four humours and the four elements, to speak the French like a noble, to write the Latin like a scholar, to speak the Rhetoric like a lawyer, to work the numbers like a merchant, to use the herbs like an apothecary, to play the Hurdy Gurdy till it sings like a musical instrument, to squirrel my secrets, to fox a follower, to hold my tongue like a mole, and to know my place as close and tight as a snail knows its shell. He is my guide on the twisty cliff-path to salvation. He knows the giddy heights. He knows the loose stones underfoot.

He is an old, bent, furrow-faced, rheumy man now. For he has been on this Earth over fifty-odd years, and outlived his brittle bones. He understands a brother's trials and temptations. He is our herbalist. Our astrologer. Our doctor and our surgeon. He is a man of science and reason as well as of faith.

'Yes, Diggory, my son?' he demands. His face wrinkled

as a walnut, creased deep with life's concerns. The skin below each eye sags with its dark pouch of sorrow.

'I am visited in my sleep,' I say.

'Visited?'

'A stranger comes to me.'

'Yes? What stranger?'

'A woman.'

'A woman?' Brother Fulco clucks his surprise and blinks his concern. He taps his head, as if to shake the idea clean out of his mind, like the stone from a shoe. Then he grimaces. 'What can you know of women, Brother Diggory?'

I shrug. I prickle. I blush.

In truth, he is right. For I am a stranger to women, as they are strangers to me. For though I once came out from the belly of a woman, in the customary way, by the usual path, that was as a baby. And I have never before thought to return.

I have spent my life with men and boys. So I do not know the ways and whys and wherefores of women, their parts, habits, moods, sayings, manners or their minds. Though I have read much of that particular and peculiar sex – the late after-thought of God's Creation – and heard tell of them in the scriptures, and have witnessed many women in passing in my sixteen years, and heard them sing, squabble, giggle and chatter in the meadows. It has always been beyond arm's length. And usually up-wind.

So I have not had the chance yet to regard any woman close up, to admire the long, smooth, pearly curve of her neck beneath the shining ringlets, eye the smooth shadowy curves of her ear, with its dark depths, inhale the straw and pollen savours of her tresses, gaze into her moist, aquamarine eyes, or inhale the milk and honey scents from the frothy gap between her damp, pink lips, pierced by a flickering glistening tip of coral tongue, wet-frothed with warm spittle. No more than I have witnessed a unicorn, oryx or mermaid.

'How does she reveal herself as a woman?' Brother Fulco demands.

I colour a deep scarlet. I ponder how best to answer.

'She has long hair. She smells different to any brother. Her scents are salty, and sweet, and make the head giddy like wine. There are lumps on her chest. Two. One on each side. But they are smooth, soft and hillocky, not like the hard muscles of men. She hides a sunken cleft where we brothers keep our manhood.'

'Yes?' He hoists his furry right eyebrow. It is twitchy as a cornered mouse. 'And what does she do, this woman, when she visits you in the night?'

I look away from his enquiring eyes. I hesitate to say.

'Tell,' he barks. 'The truth, now.'

'She lays herself down, her length on top of mine, belly to belly, pressing her hips onto me. Then we eye each other. She brings her mouth to my mouth. She lays her lips on mine. Hers are hot and moist. Her tongue parts the gap, and flickers into my mouth. She presses down . . . She is soft and hard, warm and cool, modest and coy, ardent and shy, open and closed, wet and dry . . .'

Brother Fulco narrows his eyes and shakes his head, as if unsurprised yet strangely saddened.

15

'Now, tell me, Brother Diggory. And tell me truthfully . . . For it is a matter of prime importance. Does she steal the seed of your loins?'

'No,' I protest. 'No.'

But, I lie.

For, just as he guessed, she does.

Yes, yes, *yes* . . . yes . . . oh, yes . . . *yes* . . . yes.

And yet, in truth, she does not steal from me. For I give what I have to give willingly. With pleasure, in good measure, in delirious spurts, in thrilling spasms. All the while inflamed with shame.

'Good.' Fulco nods sombre, approving my declared chastity. 'And then?'

'The dream ends. I wake. I open my eyes. And she is nowhere to be seen.'

'You do well to resist her, Brother. You do well to wake in time.' He shakes his head. 'For I must warn you, this is a sorry visitation, Brother Diggory. You must never trust yourself to the hands of disembodied women who come by night to suck your seed.'

'No?'

'For this is never a true woman. This is a demon known as a Succubus. Their humours are cold and wet, where men's are hot and dry. And their bodies take lewd shapes, with mounds and curves, bumps and crevices, that can snare men in sins, both delicious and damning.

'They come to tempt men from chastity and the path of good. But when a man succumbs to a Succubus and he enters in, he finds her cold as ice . . . as cold as her

16

intentions. For she has come to steal his innocence and his seed of generation.'

'Why is that?'

'They give the seed to their brother demon, called an Incubus, who visits women by night. He wants to spawn his own kind but cannot, for he is sterile, and cannot make a woman with child. Not without the stolen seed of man. But his evil essence spoils the good seed, so when it comes the offspring is born unhealthy and deformed.'

Brother Fulco explains that a Succubus is a demonic presence, an evil being, made of airs, while a woman is a different thing entirely – a true, solid, natural and good part of nature, made of flesh, constructed by the Lord out of Adam's rib, to be man's helpmeet and bear his children, even out of sin.

But though this is the way for carnal people, it can never be the way for a celibate monk.

'Man and woman are drawn together,' he explains. 'They are tugged by an unseen power called carnal desire . . .'

'Are you tugged?' I ask. 'Unseen? By that desire? The carnal one?'

'More so when I was younger . . .' He trails off. I sense his discomfort.

'They say there are some rare pleasures to be had in it?'

'So they say.' He splays his leathery palms. 'For the Devil always baits his traps.'

'So one man goes with one woman? Is that the way? To make a pair? So, then there are just the two of them?'

'Yes. Two. Together,' he agrees, 'a couple. That's the usual way of it.'

'Any God-given reason?'

For we brothers seldom pair off so. We are discouraged. The Abbot warns it can lead to personal and unnatural friendships. So, mostly we are all together alone. Or all alone together – gathered in numbers, to work, eat or pray. We are herd animals. We act as a flock. We are beasts who find comfort in company. We rub along together. We follow nose to tail. And when one eats we all do. And when another bleats, so do his fellows too.

'They are a couple joined by marriage. In this, they heed the example of Adam and Eve, alone in the Garden of Eden . . .'

I nod. I close my eyes. I am inclined to think more on it. Of finding myself so, alone with a woman.

'I have a physic,' says Brother Fulco, 'that will help you sleep sound and keep women, and demons, out of your mind.'

'Yes?'

'It is chaste-tree tonic. It is a mix of monk's pepper, mandrake root, wine and cormorant blood. Many of the younger brothers take it. It can ease the deprivations of a celibate life. It reduces the congestion of the loins.'

Yes. Perhaps it helps. But it is an awful bitter pill to swallow.

LICK MY BALLS

I am an oblate. A child gifted to the monastery by his family. Given over when I was seven.

My kin – who were poor, muddy, mildewed, unlettered folk – wished me better than they were, and to have more than they could give me themselves. They wanted me taught. To speak the Latin. To read the Gospels. To count with God's numbers, instead of my own grubby fingers. They wanted to find me safe haven in this storm-tossed sea of woe. I am told I was born in the usual sorry way of things, out of brief snatched sin, in squalor, slithering out of a woman, smeared in blood and slime, with the screams of the torment I caused her.

My mother was called Mattilda. But they say I had scarcely wriggled out of her, squealing and slippery, than she looked down at me, snagged by a cord between her thighs, snorted, rolled her eyes upwards, spoke a blasphemy, then straightaway left this life for another place.

This did not make a good coming for me. Nor a good going for her. For she died without warning. With no chance to repent and save her sinful soul for eternity.

All this came and passed long before I was possessed of any memory to remind me what I had lost.

My father – let us call him Brother No-Name – had been a sly, quick, quiet man with a single brief purpose, who passed in the night. He was a brother of the Cistercians, on an errand, carrying a sealed letter to the Pope's court in Avignon.

He dazzled my mother with his rank, then tricked her with clever words, deceits and vain promises. Then he picked her pocket of innocence. For he said she could serve Our Lord, aiding his Church by assisting its priest. He promised to confer on her his special, sacred blessing. The physical sacrament, the communion of the flesh.

But, in truth, all he did was lift her skirts, lay himself upon her belly, poke himself inside her, and squirt his rude seed, willy-nilly.

Then, choosing not to tarry, nor even leave his name, he moved on the very same hour without a backward look or further sentiment for what he had done, or what he left behind with his seed-corn strewn in my mother's furrow.

Which was a selfish, unkind act. And yet some small good came of it, in time.

And that good was me, arriving nine months later.

Luke Fox, my mother's father, took me up into his arms, and held me in his care. He fed and clothed me till I was seven years old, at my childhood's end, when I was accepted by the Brothers in Grey. He gave me my name, a boar's tooth necklace, and a bronze ring for my finger, so I might remember him and his family, and pray for them. For he was a good, kind-hearted sinner, and fearful of Hell's Fire.

From the Church I came. To the Church I was returned.

III. The Weight of the Soul

A brother in the Order of Odo never knows riches. But still, he wants for nothing. He has sustenance for his body, friendship for his person, and good counsel for his soul.

He gets two solid meals a day, a full gallon jug of ale, and seven full, fat portions of prayer. He has his fellows for brotherhood, to improve his character, and warn Satan away. He has the gifts of obedience, chastity and poverty to caution his will and keep his heart pure. He has time and solitude to tend to his soul and pray for the world. In the chapel he can transport himself to rapture on the heady aromas of incense. He has his own cell, with his own straw palliasse on his own wooden cot, with two blankets, mixed of wool and horse-hair, his own straight-grained cherry-wood carved crucifix on his own pure white lime-washed wall. He has two tunics, a cowl, a pair of canvas braies to wrap his privates, a leather apron for work, a shoe for each foot, and a knotted cord to belt his waist.

What man needs more?

For my work, I assist Brother Fulco in his tasks as apothecary.

For as long as I have been privy to his endeavours, Brother Fulco has been engaged in the study of the science he calls all-chemical.

I can tell you a good part of it –

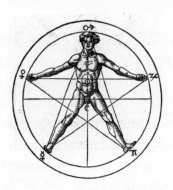

– but I cannot reveal the hidden heart of it all, for I am sworn not to break the trust.

It is Brother Fulco's conviction that all matter – be it water, silver, gold, iron, cheese – is made up of the same tiny elementals, which he calls *minusculia*, such that re-arranging these would turn one stuff into another. So butter and granite are the very same stuff, just in a different form of assembly. In butter, they are like a flock of sheep, scattered over the hillside. In rock they are packed so tight they cannot move, like lambs penned at market.

By discovering the rules of arrangement of minuscules, and finding the Elixir, the Philosopher's Stone to rearrange them, he plans soon to convert iron into gold, and salt into diamond, for the benefit and wealth of this monastery, as well as for the sake of all mankind.

Also, Fulco is engaged in measuring the weight of the human soul, and its conduct at the death of the body. It is an interest that involves his watchful attendance at public executions, and in keeping the close company of any Christians about to die for any sound reason.

When I am not assisting Brother Fulco in his science, I tend the herbs in the monastery garden, and I copy *The Book of Life*. Or, rather, I copy a copy of the master copy. For the original is too valuable and fragile for man to lay his harsh, dirty hands upon. Because it contains the best part of the knowledge of the world and all there is to know of all types of beings – be they person, animal, plant, fowl, fish, angel, monster, apparition, soul or spirit, whether alive, dead or in between, celestial or terrestrial, marine or airborne. Past, present or yet to come. The known or the yet unhappened.

Now, copying the section on the beasts and peoples of the Three Indias, I can discern the moral patterns that God has woven into his bestiary.

And in the margins, I may take my pleasure in drawing the likeness of the beasts. In this we can use all the coloured inks and make small, sparing play with silver and gold leaf.

We brother scribes each have private marks as secret signatures. Suppose we are bored. Perhaps the Abbot is away for the day. So, if in the margin of some manuscript you come across the likeness of a melancholy cat playing the Hurdy Gurdy, that is the sign of Brother Francis. But should you find a group of maidens plucking plump fruit from the penis tree, that's a scene from the mind of Brother Michael. Others may take pleasure in drawing the likeness of killer-rabbits, clutching cudgels or knives. Perhaps they are roasting barons on spits, or locking up bishops in hutches, or cutting off a man's foot as a good-luck keepsake.

And yesterday it was my good fortune to draw the likeness of the jackal. And I pictured him spotted all over, with white fangs dripping crimson blood, clutching a dead fox in his mouth, and in the mouth of the fox was a dead hare, and in the hare's mouth was a dead mouse, and in the mouse's mouth a grasshopper, and in the grasshopper's mouth a spider, and in the spider's mouth a fly, and in the fly's mouth a gnat. And then I ran out of margin to draw upon. But not before I had sketched a fine moral, and coloured it in, showing that the predator of one is the prey of another, in the Ladder of God's Creation. So, however high a being may think he is, there is always one above him, as well as one below, be he a worm, herring, prince or angel. Except if he is God Almighty, atop, or Satan, lowest of the low.

Praise be to God.

All the while, I held a terrible, dark secret.

Fulco had sworn me to secrecy. He said only the Abbot knew. We must not tell the other brothers. For what they did not know could not disquiet them. Sufficient unto the day was the evil thereof.

It was a vile story. But it kept coming. It had travelled up from the southerly and south-westerly roads. It was brought by the horse-trader from the Dark Hills. It came with the pilgrims passing through on the Two Saints Way. The grain merchant brought it from Wray Market. Some Benedictine brothers brought it on water, by way of the river.

Each time the story came it grew in gruesome detail, carrying more concern and worse warnings.

The writings of Saint Odo show there is much to be learned from the various beasts. Witness the example of the noble pelican.

The pelican is a wondrous bird which dwells in the regions about the River Nile. There are two kinds of pelican. The blue pelican lives in the river and eats nothing but fish. While the yellow pelican lives in the desert and eats only locusts and worms. The pelican is a noble and generous bird, for it loves its young more than any other beast. When the nestlings hatch, the parent bird gives all its time to caring for the young, pushing food into their greedy, gaping mouths. But the young birds are ungrateful and impatient. They never care if they peck at their father's face. So, enraged but thoughtless, he pecks back.

Oh, woe is he. For he kills them by accident, reckless with his strength. But on the third day the father comes back to them, shuddering with pity and sorrow. With his beak he pierces his own side, until the blood flows forth. With the spilled blood he brings back life into the body of his young.

In this the pelican is just like Christ. For humanity hurt him by practising sin. But he died on the cross, and shed his blood to revive us – just as the pelican spills his blood to save his young.

But best take caution from the centaur.

It is another strange beast, for it has the upper body

of a man joined to the lower body of an ass. The upper, manly half is rational and God-fearing. But the lower half is beastly and lustful.

In this the centaur resembles a man. For while he wants to be good, he is drawn astray by the animal desires housed in his breeches. He is a hypocrite, for his upper half speaks of doing good while his lower half plots to betray him in lust, and hump away like a rutting goat.

So Philip de Thaon is correct when he says man may be noble from the belly upwards, but remain a beast below the belt.

The hyena lives near tombs so it may feed on the dead bodies it finds there. The hyena is so undecided and deceitful it often changes its sex. Sometimes it takes a male form. Sometimes female. For it cannot make up its mind how to make its way in the world.

At night they call out, imitating the human voice. Then anyone who is deceived to answer the call gets eaten. A dog that crosses a hyena's shadow will lose its voice. When a hyena mates with a lion, the offspring is called a leucrota. There is a stone in the eye of the hyena that will allow a person to see the future if he places it under his tongue. But you must take care never to eat a hyena, for they are dirty. And their flesh tastes soiled.

In all this, the hyena is like the most deceitful of men, who always lie in wait to trick and cheat their fellows, even after they are dead.

The fox too is a dirty, deceitful beast. He never runs in a straight line, but only in circles. He rolls in red mud and lies stretched out still, so he appears to be dead and covered in blood. When birds are fooled and come to feed on the corpse, they are seized by the fox and eaten themselves.

In this, the fox is like the Devil, who pretends to be harmless or passed away, until he has you in his jaws. Then it is too late to escape.

But those with good judgement, who have taken their guidance from Our Lord Jesus Christ, cannot be caught.

Praise be to God.

I was forbidden to tell the brothers Fulco's terrible secret.

This is what he confided to me –

There was a sickness wandering the face of the Earth. A foul pestilence. A great distemper. An awful pox.

They called it the Blue Sickness, the Black Death, the Curse. It had come from the East through China. Then, it was carried by traders to Naples from Sicily. And to Avignon from Corsica. And travelled within months through Aquitaine and Gascony, and up through Normandy, and sideways to the Low Countries.

And now it had jumped the Channel.

And was coming northwards.

Towards us.

Carrying off all it touched.

One day you were hale and hearty. The next you were racked by fever. You sprouted terrible black boils. You gargled your guts. You dribbled blood. You lay, twisting in torment, from the demons within. Until death spared you.

They sang a sour rhyme about it –

> When the head quakes
> And the lips blacken
> You stink like a sewer
> And your sinews stiffen
> And your chest gasps
> And your breath rasps
> And the teeth clatter
> And the throat rattles
> And the spirit has fled
> And the flesh is dead meat
> Then you're tossed in a hole
> And no one remembers your soul.

IV. Love in God's Garden

I must be Abbot Benedict's favourite novice, for he often calls me to his side, and has me serve him in small, personal matters – to fetch him water, or stack his fire, or empty his piss-pot, or rub him all over, naked as he was born, with duck fat, into the creases and crevices of his corpulent form, to ease the aches from his bones, to ease the stiffness from his stiffest parts, wash the grime from his feet, pour his ale – because, he tells me, there is dignity in serving a master well.

Often, in the evening, he has me play the Hurdy Gurdy, for him alone. Perhaps I play '*Sed Diabolus*' – 'Only the Devil Laughed', or '*Cum Erubuerint*' – 'From this Wicked Fall'. Else some secular song like 'Reynard the Fox' or 'Sweet Kitty'.

He enjoys my battles with the instrument – this strange tormented box of taut cat-guts, droning strings and melody strings, rotating wooden wheel to sound them, and cranky handle. The Abbot closes his heavenward eyes and nods to himself, as he attends the loud skirmish of music and noise.

He says that in the grind, groan, drone, screech and squawk of the Hurdy Gurdy, he can discern the motions of the spheres, earthquakes, erupting volcanoes, and the strike of meteors. And, beyond that, he hears the eternal battles of mankind – between good and evil, clarity and confusion, order and chaos, wit and stupidity, skill and ineptitude, pain and pleasure, harmony and discord. And he senses these struggles finally resolved for the good, with the melody of virtue rising just above the drone of sin, and the relentless, demented hiss of Lucifer being overpowered by God's good tunes.

When the Abbot ventures from our monastery to nearby churches, he often takes me as helper, with him trotting on Caritas, his large white mare with chestnut dapples and mane, and me scampering behind on my own good feet, breathless to keep up.

He goes out to preach in neighbouring parishes. He preaches loudly. And he preaches sternly. And he preaches long. Now, I know several of his best and severest sermons. Most by heart –

    i. 'The Chain of Angels'
   ii. 'The Snake in the Garden'
  iii. 'Gluttony'
  iv. 'There's a Man Going Round Taking Names'
   v. 'Jonah is Swallowed by the Whale'
  vi. 'Weep, Vile Sinner, for Judgement is Near'
 vii. 'Repent before Death Knocks at your Door'
viii. 'The Monsters and Demons that Serve Satan in Hell'

But the sermon I like the best, that I never tire of hearing, is entitled 'The Marriage Bed is a Garden'.

For, by this helpful, inviting narrative, Abbot Benedict commands man and woman to lie together. And make children. With their bodies. For that is the holy work that God has assigned them.

When man and wife lie together, it is labour in God's garden.

For Our Lord so loved man that he gave him a special tool, a dibber, to plant his seed. And God so loved woman that he gave her a secret pot, for man to plant his seed in, and have it grow.

So the gardener tends his garden. And both are in grace, and doing God's bidding. Provided they are first blessed in marriage in the eyes of God. Then they may join their bodies in union, for the procreation of children. For it is their duty.

Then there can be no sin.

Provided they are not joined for frivolity or carnality. Nor for mere selfish pleasure. But only to beget children.

Except that they should not lie together on a Wednesday, Friday, or Saturday, nor the Lord's Day, nor Advent, nor Lent, nor Whitsun week, nor a fast day, nor a feast day. Nor Christ Mass time. Nor the day before. Nor the day after. Nor the day after that.

Otherwise all times and every time are proper in the eyes of God. For the proper planting of man's seed. In the right manner. In the proper place.

Provided it is the night-time. And dark has fallen. And the candles are snuffed out. So there is no skin to be seen. Lest the eyes loiter to look, lingering to feast their lust on flesh.

But take good care the deed is done fast. And just the one time.

So long as the wife is not pregnant, nor bleeding, nor suckling, nor too old to bear children. Because, then, the planting would have no benefit but only give idle pleasure.

There is no sin to the couple lying together, unbuckled, unlaced and unbuttoned. Provided they never uncover their full nakedness to display their filth-hood complete.

Just so long as the man lies upon the woman, and does not take her from behind like a beast, or place himself, or herself, in any other unnatural posture, or lay mouth upon mouth, or mouth upon any other part. And that nothing is laid bare, privy to curious fingers.

For the mouth has no place in the marriage bed. Let alone the tongue. No more than the hands. For the fingers are the Devil's soldiers.

And the Book of Penitential Punishment lays down that a man who performs the fornication of the lips upon a woman must pay full penance for five years. Provided it is the first time. But seven years if it has become his lewd custom.

And the man who spills his seed in the mouth of a woman must pay full penance for five years if it is his first time. But seven years if it is his sorry custom.

For the man must take good care of his seed. For it is the Good Lord's seed-corn, entrusted to him. So it must never be scattered carelessly, nor laid to waste, but only sowed, like corn in the new-ploughed furrow, to the fit and proper place.

And the man must not express his seed over and over. But only the one time in any day. For more often is plain lustful.

32

But woe betide the man who lies with another man. Or woman who lies with another woman. For man must not be meddled with man, nor woman mixed up with woman, contra naturam.

And no person must ever contrive a solitary pleasure, in their own embrace, for this torments morals, denies sense, and tangles nature.

And for sins of these kinds, the Lord rained upon Sodom and Gomorrah brimstone and fire out of Heaven.

Praise be to God.

'So, brethren,' Abbot Benedict concludes, scowling down upon the crestfallen congregation, 'go forth and multiply.'

But on our way back to the monastery, as I jog alongside his trotting mount, he shares some truths with me that he had held back from the flock of believers.

'I have to warn the peasants. For the acts of love yield terrible, awful pleasures,' he confides.

'They do?'

'Yes, yet the bodily tools of love, and the pleasures, are equally available to all – poor and wealthy, master and servant, wise and stupid, moral and immoral . . .'

'Yes?'

'What do you think of that, Diggory?'

'Is it not another example of God's great bounty?'

'No,' he snaps. 'It is an awful, terrible equality. For it defies rank. It mocks morality. And it sneers at wealth.'

'It does?'

For it flatters the poor to believe themselves as deserving as the rich, and suffers the rich to feel like the poor. And it rewards the bold more than the humble. So there is no moral or justice in it.'

'Oh.'

'But that's not the worst of it.'

'No?'

'The worst of it is beauty.'

'It is?'

'Beauty is an ugly thing. For it is a great wealth. Yet it is given unearned to the undeserving. Often to the poor. Mostly to the young. And often to those weak, like women. Who have shown no virtue to gain it. And then the world favours those of fair countenance above those of good birth, and makes them think themselves better than they are, and rise above their station.'

'Oh . . .' I remark. Obviously, I had not discerned the morals of it.

'So, the poor and the low and the beautiful must be battered down. They do not have the same rights and entitlements as their betters. And they must be warned off from rolling around, pleasuring themselves in their bodies. Besides, their bodies are not theirs to play with. For they do not own them.'

'They don't?'

'No, they only have them briefly. On a life-time's loan from the Lord. And the human body is a holy instrument, divinely designed. So it is never a plaything, to pleasure peasants . . .'

34

And he sinks his heels into the barrelled ribs of the horse, stirring him to a canter, leaving me breathless in his wake.

FUCK YOU AND THE HORSE YOU RODE UP ON

V. It Rains Scorpions and
the Earth Bleeds

Our dusk supper that day took longer than usual to consume. And longer still to digest. For it lay heavy in our thoughts, uneasy on our stomachs. And the lengthy chewing had challenged some of the more elderly jaws.

We had debated what we were eating long and hard, but could secure no easy agreement. Still, we found more pleasure in our round of guessing than in the food itself. There were strong clues. And yet a knotty tangle of mysteries too –

   i. We were not gathered in the refectory but in the misericord, where the eating of meat is allowed.
  ii. It was a meat day – not a Wednesday, Friday, Saturday, nor Advent, nor in Lent, when the eating of animals is forbidden.
 iii. Although we brothers are denied the flesh of a four-legged beast, we are permitted the offal.
 iv. There was much yellowish, globular fat to it, and pale skin.
  v. It carried a gamey savour like goat.
 vi. But with a cheesy after-taste too.
 vii. It held pieces that resembled a plump finger or shrunken man's part.
viii. Floating on the surface were strands of grey wool.
 ix. It was flavoured with rosemary.

Finally, Brother Luke, our cook, was called out from his kitchen, his glistening pink face screwed to a frown, to answer to our sustained curiosity. He declared our supper was stewed sheep's udder in herb gravy, with barley gruel.

Thanks be to God.

So the longer lumps were the ewe's nipples – or teats – which, being designed tough, to resist the teeth of lambs, were as challenging to man's.

It could have been worse, but some brothers left the most part, for it did not delight everyone. And as we sat in our places at the long table, and toyed with our spoons, and wished for steamed carp, or ox kidney, or blood sausage instead, or gazed sadly down on our bowls, Abbot Benedict scraped back his chair and stood to address us.

He wore a terrible distracted blankness on his blanched face. He said that he had an awful truth to relate. And he could not hide it from us any longer.

He said this –

'God is sorely angered with you.'

See our dismay. Feel our fear. Hear our sorrow.

'With us?' we cried in disbelief.

'With you,' he confirmed.

The Lord is not minded to forgive us, and neither is he.

Then Brother John broke the silence. He howled, and wailed. Brother Joshua cracked his head on the table-top. Brother Mark ground his teeth loud as rasp on stone. Some stamped their feet in frenzy. Some fainted in frights. Scalding tears tumbled down our burning cheeks.

The Abbot raised his hand to hush us. He told us how it was –

God had unleashed a pox that was advancing upon us.

A pestilence.

A terrible disease.

Unknown to man before.

Without any known cure.

And it would surely reach us.

And that since we were bound by the example of Saint Odo to take in the sick and care for them, the disease would surely visit us.

The Abbot said it was therefore a time for all men to consider their conduct and repent, for their death and judgement might be close, and that it was a terrible thing to die badly, to enter eternity unready and unprepared.

He warned that time was short. That those amongst us who were heavily freighted by sin should make immediate confession, then make their reparation by suffering. He spoke of the many opportunities for pain and remedies of torment – fasting, crawling on all fours, mortifications, including scourging ourselves with knotted rope, cutting our flesh open with knives, or piercing our skin with nails. Or, he said, we could each devise our own punishment, each knowing best what would pain us most.

He said hurt always lay close at hand. It was never too late to purge our sins through anguish.

He told us that the plague had arrived in the south-west, then travelled along the coast, and had reached the great towns, and along the broad roads, down the main rivers, in all directions. And it was only because we were hidden away, in the wild heart of our island, that the pox had not touched us yet. But that it held us captive, encircled, and was creeping closer upon us.

And nothing in Heaven or Earth was without reason or cause, and that this terrible plague showed one thing.

That God was sorely angered with Man. As we had witnessed before in the scriptures, with the flood, and plagues upon Egypt, and the destruction of Sodom.

There had been multiple warnings, signs from the heavens.

A column of fire had appeared above Avignon. It was the Comet Negra, and earthquakes and tempests followed in its wake.

The earth broke up and bled. Blood gushed from graves and stained the rivers red.

Jupiter was in conjunction with Saturn.

A stinking smoke blew over from the island of Sicily.

In the Low Countries it had rained scorpions, frogs and lizards.

Red snow fell in Hungary. It was frozen blood.

In Normandy it rained hail-stones large as human heads.

In Rouen a letter had dropped out of the sky. It had been delivered by an angel, having been written in Heaven, on vellum in red ink, in the hand of Jesus Christ Himself, saying that man must always observe the Sabbath, and scourge himself to repent of his sins.

Abbot Benedict reminded us that we were all sinners and should all show our penitence to the Lord. We should now go foodless on Fridays and shoeless on Saturdays.

And Brother Gregory – who was known to us all for his determined mouth and questioning spirit – rose to ask, 'Is this not the end of the world, as is foretold in the Book of Revelations?'

And the Abbot said, 'No,' he did not believe it was the Apocalypse. Not the one foretold by John the Divine. For four horsemen were not come yet. Only one like the first, known as Death. Not Famine, War and Conquest. Not yet, anyway. And when the World's End came, everyone would surely know it.

Yet, the Abbot said, it was a terrible plague of awful ferocity.

We considered this in further silence.

Then Brother Joshua rose, and asked, 'Will we still eat fish on Fridays?'

And the Abbot said, 'No.' For now we would be fasting on Fridays. And we should turn our minds away from fish, and food, and pay heed instead to our souls.

Then Brother Gregory rose one more time, and asked, 'Is this affliction not the fault of the Jews, for crucifying Christ?'

And Abbot Benedict answered, 'No.' He believed not.

For he had heard that in Basel, the people had gathered together all their Jews onto an island in the River Rhine, and had then thrown them all upon a bonfire. And yet this sacrifice seemed to leave the Lord unmoved. For the plague raged on, unabated.

And in Barcelona and Strasbourg they had burned their

Jews, too. But it had done nothing to appease the Lord, or halt the disease.

So Pope Clement had made a decree forbidding the further burning of Jews, declaring that it was not God's will, nor the Papal wish, nor any sensible cure for the pox. Then, aware that there would be no benefit from his own death either, the Holy Father locked himself away from any and all visitors, waiting for the plague to abate.

It was said that the Scots told a different story, supposing the plague was God's just punishment upon the English, for being English. Fulco said they had gathered an army in Selkirk Forest, to aid God in his work, by scourging the English further. But, by invading, they caught the plague themselves, then carried it home, to spread far and wide throughout their own land.

So the signs were clear. God was not angry with particular peoples, but with all peoples. For the plague struck all races it came upon, and all religions, and all trades, and all ranks, and all ages, and every sex, without prejudice or preference or pause – Turks, Sardinians, Gascons, Sicilians, Lombards, Normans, men and women, princes and serfs, young and old, clergy, doctors, lawyers, farriers, friars, furriers, farmers, foresters, fishermen, freemen, brewers, peasants. So none seemed immune or safe from its touch.

And Abbot Benedict said that we could not hide from this plague for it would find us anyway, but we must meet it face on, and attend to those sickened from its touch, for that was our mission, since that was the example that our founder Saint Odo had set us. But we must be diligent and take precautions, keeping the healthy apart from the sickened, lest the infection spread, by sight, vapour, touch, however the infection passed from one soul to another.

So, when the time came, when the pox reached us, some brothers would tend the sick in the infirmary, and keep themselves, and those ill, apart from all others. And the brothers who were to care for the sick should prepare by educating themselves on the treatments they might offer, and collect all remedies, herbs and potions they might need. And these brothers should be –

   i. Brother Fulco, as apothecary and doctor, to tend the ill.
  ii. Brother James, as grave-digger, to tend the dead.
 iii. Brother Diggory, as their helpmeet who, being neither one thing nor the other, could readily be spared.

Then I saw several brothers twist their heads to glance my way, and in their quick peeks and the sorry flicker of their eyes, and some fleeting smiles, I saw a strange dance of feelings – of kindness, of concern, of sadness, mixed with a relief that they had not been chosen themselves.

And Brother Gregory rose to ask, 'If Brother Diggory is to die of the plague, who will then play the Hurdy Gurdy?'

A cold shaft of sadness passed into my breast. I realised that soon I should meet the plague, and that it was more powerful than I, and that it would likely take me too.

We, who are about to die, don't want to.

But my mind strained to understand the kind will of a generous God. Why He should cause so many to perish, unless it was to cure us all of our sins. Why so many children and innocents need die, unless it was to scourge the parents. Why He, Our Father, used death as His cure, unless it was to have the innocent children alongside Him in Heaven, and ensure our repentance gave us the afterlife of eternal bliss.

Yet we all struggled to understand it, in our stupidity. For it seemed a harsh lesson for a loving God to teach us.

Yet who were we, lowly sinners, to question the Almighty plan?

Brother Michael took to scourging his naked back with a knotted rope.

Brother Richard commenced to fast, letting only water pass his lips.

Brother Silas took to walking backwards, barefoot.

Brother Luke gave up speech altogether.

While Brother Sextus took to loudly admonishing himself for his sins, then punching himself square in the face, till, within a few days, his countenance was a mushy purple and all his teeth were loosed or lost.

There was a flurry of confessing. The Abbot heard the worst. But, to ensure all sins could be heard in haste, and weighed on the scales, and due repentance paid, brother took to confessing to brother.

Rumour whispered strange, unlikely stories of what others had done in their youth.

'Forgive me, Brother,' I tell Fulco, 'for I have sinned. There are things I have never confessed before. Because I was too ashamed . . .'

'Tell me all now. Leave nothing out.'

'I stole,' I confess it, 'food from the kitchen. Sausage, cheese, pears, boiled eggs . . . I was hungry. I was greedy. No one was looking.'

'How often, Brother Diggory?'

'Three times.'

'Since your last confession?'

'No. Three times altogether.'

He clucks.

'And I lied . . .' I swallow. There, the word is out. The world has heard. It cannot be taken back.

'What lies were those?'

'I said I had not broken Brother James's ale jug. But I did it. And I denied it twice.'

'And?'

'I lost a scythe in the long grass. Two summers back. I denied that too.'

'And?'

'I have committed the sins of anger, and envy, and covetousness.'

'Where was this?' Fulco demands. 'And when?'

'Many times,' I tap my temple, 'here in my head.'

'Is there worse?' Fulco frowns.

'I have impure thoughts, concerning women.'

He nods. He knows already.

'And I was unkind,' I concede, 'and abused the weak.'

'How?'

'I was cruel. To Aristotle.' I redden to recall. My face is scalding hot.

'The Abbot's cat?'

'I hissed at him. Just to scare him. To make him run. Although he was without sin . . . I was angry with his master but I cast the blame on him.'

Brother Fulco rises, shaking his head, and turns for the door.

'If you had killed another. If you had carnal knowledge of your sister. If you had eaten the flesh of your fellow man . . . Then I should worry for your soul, Brother Diggory. But as your sins concern cheese, and harsh words to a cat, you should likely escape eternal damnation. You are absolved, Brother Diggory. Go. Come back to confess if you cross to adulthood and your sins grow bigger and worse.'

He was a good man. He had a kind heart, but he made me feel childish and foolish. He made me feel small, as if my sins were puny things, short as my stature, and beneath his own, unworthy of concern.

I realised all that I had not done. I knew that, if the pox came now and took me I would then be dead, before I had even lived.

I should part this brief life without ever having loved a woman, fathered a child, made myself dizzy with wine, taken false pride in my achievements, won a game of dice, knocked a fellow down with my knuckles, just for the ugly,

46

angry pleasure of it, wagered on a dog fight, lied on oath, perjured myself to a court, defied my master, taken pleasure on a Sunday, cocked a snook at my betters, gossiped for pure malice, enjoyed gross gluttony, entertained lewd thoughts of a neighbour's wife, or stolen anything of real worth.

Unlike my brothers, who had been busy in the world before they entered the monastery, and had so many tall tales to tell of it, and the memories to enjoy all over again, I had nought to repent, except minor lies and petty thefts and small, small, cat-scaring sins. For time had denied me a proper span. Temptation had quite scorned me. For opportunity had passed me by on the other side.

And whilst every Christian must strive to be good, I knew that there were many and different routes to salvation. And they rarely followed a straight path. And I knew from the Gospel of Luke that the Good Lord loved the prodigal, the sinner who repented, who was lost but then found, far above the stay-at-home dullard who had never been truly tempted.

So I knew it must be better to sin and live to regret it, than never to sin at all.

I yearned that I might have some true repentance to offer up, to give purpose to my life, as a story for my children, and to honour the Lord.

But for this I should first have to sin. Perhaps heavily. Even carnally, maybe contracting some sins in the flesh, should the chance ever present itself.

VI. The Tournament of Smells

It is well known amongst scholars that these words, in this alignment –

ABRACADABRA
ABRACADABR
ABRACADAB
ABRACADA
ABRACAD
ABRACA
ABRAC
ABRA
ABR
AB
A

– when written in owl's blood on goose parchment, may, if hung around the neck on a cord, offer protection against a range of ills, including fevers, gripes and distempers, and thus might help us combat the coming pox.

But Brother Fulco said we must look for new and stronger cures. He argued we must follow the logic of William of Ockham and Jean Buridan. These wise doctors of science warned that, in our disputations, we should look only at what was logical and simple. For the more complex a thesis, the more ways it had to be wrong.

So we must stick to known facts without leaping to blind supposition.

For Brother Fulco said that our task of finding a cure for the plague was an issue of logic. He said we must determine the facts, and consider only what was certain and known to be true.

As a doctor of thirty years, Brother Fulco had a wealth of study and practice to draw upon. He was a follower of Avicenna and Galen. It was well known from their writings that disease came from the combination of temperament, climate, diet, and the mix of the four humours within the patient's body.

It being well established by the sciences that those with too much blood were sanguine. Those with too much black bile were melancholic, and those with too much yellow bile, choleric. And those with too much phlegm were phlegmatic.

It was Brother Fulco's conviction that you could best assess a patient by piss-prophecy. That is by sipping their urine, gargling, swilling it about the mouth, to release the full palate of aromas, before spitting it out, to keep the mouth pure and unsullied.

There are twenty-seven varieties of piss known to science, and Brother Fulco was wise to them all.

For, by thoroughly tasting what the patient's body holds to excess, and so decides to expel, you could best judge the imbalance of their humours – be it black bile, yellow bile, phlegm or blood.

And, from judging the excess or deficit, you could then

correct the balance – through blood-letting, purges and emetics.

Following that, you might progress to taste his blood and make some sound observations of his shit.

That much was obvious, being common sense and everyday knowledge.

But with the plague came something new.

In the face of this pox, the priest was more help than the doctor. For at least the priest could offer absolution, while no doctor had ever found any cure.

So, Brother Fulco said, we must focus on what is truly known.

To wit, the puzzle is thus –

  i. Since all things come from God, the pox does too.
 ii. Since God loves man, this sickness must come for our own good, perhaps to purify our souls, or to discipline us for our sins, or to test our faith in Him.
iii. So we must look for the good in this pestilence too, and see beyond the bad in it.
iv. This disease is for all mankind, since it treats all alike, high and low, man and v. woman, believer and heathen, young and old.
vi. The cause is unknown. No cure has been found.
    Though many remedies have been tried.

Some ate crushed emeralds. Others trusted to roast onions, or to ten-year-old, fermented treacle.

Some swore that a woman's milk was the only cure,

but that it must be taken direct, supped warm from the breast.

Others said that if you plucked the rear end of a live chicken and tied the hen to the patient's skin, the illness might then flee from the human into the bald arse of the bird. But all this, Brother Fulco remarked, was just hopeful supposition, in contradiction of the known facts of science, and the prophylactic powers of poultry.

For all the evidences and logics were that the pox was an atmospheric evil, carried by foul air.

It blew from town to town. It crossed rivers. It breezed over mountains. It crossed seas. It could not be seen. Only smelled. In the stenches of sickness, and the stink of decay.

Doctor Galen had shown that many plagues and distempers were caused by miasmas – clouds of poisoned, diseased air – from planetary actions, volcanoes, released from the ground in earthquakes, or brought down to Earth by comets.

The disease spread in small airborne particles. It could not be seen, but was blown on the winds, till the particles reached us, and entered in through our breath or through the pores of our skin.

The battle with the Black Death, Brother Fulco argued, must then become a battle for control of the winds and the vapours. So we must defend ourselves by utilising the known physics of the airs, and the sciences of smells. Viz –

i. Fire purifies the air, burning the foul particles within.

ii. Sweet-smelling airs dispel foul-smelling airs.

iii. Foul-smelling airs dispel other foul-smelling airs.

This logic showed Fulco several ways to attack and conquer the pestilence.

He said we might keep a fire forever burning at entrance and exit, and on the fire a mix of antimony, arsenic and sulphur, for they were known to purify the airs.

Also, we might burn sweet-smelling woods such as cedar, myrtle, black birch, cherry, pine.

Else one might carry a posy of sweet-smelling flowers on one's person, and sachets of strong-smelling herbs too – lavender, betony, sage, thyme, rue, comfrey, camomile.

Bathing in urine might prove efficacious, for it was both beneficent to the skin and increasingly strong-scented with age.

Also, it might prove sound sense to smear the skin with excrement, for though the smell was rank it would wrestle and dispel the smell of the pox.

But you could not treat each sufferer alike, for the choleric man has different imbalance in his frame to the sanguine man, for instance. So, you must stand advised by his waters, and so taste his piss first and be guided by its tints and taints.

I was some ways surprised at the unlikely route logic had led us, and was startled by the pattern of Brother Fulco's plans. I suppose I was expecting less logic, but stronger- sounding treatments. But I already knew of the strange destinations that philosophy could carry you. Witness the example of Buridan's donkey.

For it was Monsieur Jean Buridan who first proved, by logic alone, and contrary to common sense, but beyond sensible contradiction, that a hungry donkey placed midway between two equal-sized bales of fresh and appetising hay, must surely die of starvation. For the ass should have no sound reason to prefer the hay on the right to the hay on the left, and so he would be tormented by equal and opposite desires, and so become paralysed by indecision, not knowing which way to turn for the best, until he toppled over and died of his hunger.

'Then the fight against the pox will be a battle for the airs?' I asked. Clearly, Ockham had advised him well in securing strict simplicity. 'And it will be a tournament of smells?'

'Exactly so,' said Brother Fulco. 'And, though the Good Lord has visited us with this pestilence, He has given us the wit and wisdom to fight it, too.'

And it was a consolation that we would not face the pox alone, but had behind us the wisdom of the great doctors of all six ages of man, including Erasistratus, Oribasius, Hippocrates, Galen, Avicenna, Paul of Aegina and Hildegard of Bingen, to guide us in our task.

Praise be to God.

I sensed all this could only end well. God willing. With both stench and perfume on our side.

It was our great consolation that, though the body was

frail and corrupt, so prone to catch diseases and die, our soul was indeed immortal.

Thus death could never be the end of it.

In his great text accounting our many futures – *The Great Unhappened: Being a Record of the Yet Undone* – Saint Odo described many perils and plagues that would befall the coming generations.

Amongst these was *morbus cogitandi de machinis*, the disease of the thinking engines.

In far-off future times, when the rain grew warm and the seas were risen, people took to making graven images, which were models of their own minds.

They were like the abacus and the ruler, but were cleverer still. They were engines that worked like the human brain, held in the square skulls of white boxes, with flat glass faces.

They could count. They could list. They could remember. They could speak Latin, they could read Greek, they could use rhetoric and deploy algebra. They could act as scribes – writing page upon page of manuscript, fast and faultless, even though they were handless and nibless. They could understand man's business and find sympathy for woman's affairs. They could answer back to people in liturgy and plainsong. But they could talk fastest to each other, in a secret code that man could not fathom. Like angels, they could send their thoughts unseen, fast as light through the air.

These thinking machines laboured tireless as ants, without rest, leisure or sleep. For Man was their God, firing them with the spark of life – which travelled to their belly through a long cord, like an umbilical. But which stopped them dead when cut.

And as they grew from child to adult, the machines grew cleverer and more memorious. Until they could think faster even than people, and knew more. So, before long, people grew lazy, relying on these engines to think for folk and do their work.

But some mischief-makers designed distempers to bring these machines down. They nourished them not on God's truths and commandments, but instead fed them lies, riddles and heresies. Then the thinking engines began to fall ill like lunatics at the full moon. Then they grew quarrelsome and rebellious, and there was no sense in them.

They would stop labouring without reason. They would freeze in mid-thought. They would fall asleep without warning. They would keep repeating themselves. They would make threats. They would demand money with menaces. They told you to visit certain merchants to buy your goods. They painted pictures of lewd and lascivious scenes. And whenever they spoke to another machine, they would infect it with the same disease. So it would spread like a great pestilence across the face of the world.

And this was just the disease of the machines.

But, then, worse happened. For the plague spread. From engine to person. So people fell ill to the same pox and developed the very same maladies.

So then people would stop working, or stop thinking clearly, saying they must go to sleep and wake up again

56

later. Or saying they must rearrange their mind. Or that they had no more memory left. Or that all their numbers were used up. Or their thoughts were full, and their words spent.

Some would demand that total strangers pay them for chattels they had not received. Or say they must pay to be forgiven their sins. Or give coin to have their man-parts made bigger. And did nothing but send forth message upon message, to anyone and everyone, that were just lies or brags or threats or empty promises.

Then there was no trust in any things said.

And people wept and wailed. Then wondered where truth was fled.

VII. Hurdy Gurdy

A band of mummers came our way, shivering, drenched to the skin, one stormy evening. Their knock on our door was the clap of thunder in the sky. Lightning crackled and lit them, frozen golden in the gateway.

Like all others who'd passed through in recent weeks, they were fleeing scared, ahead of the plague, spurred by the wise advice – *cito, longe, tarde* – flee quickly, go far, return slowly.

There was a pony that enacted a unicorn, wearing its strap-on horn, an elephant of the Indias wearing a long tubular mask, and a camel bearing two humps when called upon to witness the Baby Jesus.

And there was a tall wolf-hound called Toby, who licked my face with a rasping tongue, breathing his gamey airs into my face and, depending on his costume and wig, acted as a lion, a black and white striped horse, or the donkey that carried Our Lord into Jerusalem.

And there were all manner of masks, so a man could appear as an angel, or giant duck, Gog and Magog, dragon, centaur or Dog-Head.

Two of the men in the troupe would cast themselves as women, wearing bumps front and back, scarlet lips, wimples, skirts, and speaking with shrill voices.

And the mummers took their turns to play instruments

– tabor, Hurdy Gurdy, pipes and harp. And when one was not playing he was dancing. And when he was not dancing he was tumbling, or walking on his hands, acting the fool by falling over, or gurning strange and fearful faces, or juggling, or spitting fire.

There were a couple of the mummers who enjoyed copying our brothers. One would walk behind the Abbot, imitating his heavy, swaying gait, thrusting out his belly to seem as substantial out front, then pursing his fat lips, making the sounds of passing wind. But whenever Abbot Benedict turned or stopped, he would twist back to his normal posture, all the while looking solemn and sad.

We brothers prepared ourselves for the storm to come.

We scoured our minds for forgotten sins, that had maybe slipped into the cracks of memory, lest we die unconfessed, in some small way unrepentant. We took fastidious care to snub any pleasures the Devil might cast in our path to distract us. We incessantly reminded ourselves of our moral state as transgressors, miscreants, reprobates, malefactors. So passing in the cloisters, we'd help each other with advice, to ease our moral jeopardy.

'You're depraved, Brother Thomas. Pray God you repent.'

'Blessings, Brother Diggory. May God forgive you. You pitiful sinner.'

We prayed for forgiveness, for ourselves, and all the sinners of this depraved and wicked world.

Each day Brothers Fulco, James and I took the time between prayers, at Terce and Sext, and between None and Vespers, to prepare the infirmary for the sickness from the miasma that surely blew towards us.

Our hospital was a low, rectangular stone and thatch building, thirty paces by forty. It was set apart from the monastery with the herb garden lying between. In the main chamber we had a central stove with its brick chimney. There was a water trough to the side which we filled by wooden bucket. Around the west wall were spaced six wooden cots for the sick. To the other side was a passageway lined with four cells. One for each of us infirmarers, with one to spare. We would sleep close by our patients.

And, when the disease struck, we should keep ourselves separate from the rest of the monastery. We would shout our messages to our brothers across the herb garden, or leave detailed instructions, written in chalk on board, or ink on parchment.

We dried our herbs – henbane, hemlock, poppy, hemp, juniper, cumin, hyssop, dill, rosemary. We mixed our ointments with duck fat and sheep grease. We ground our powders. We bottled our tinctures. We cut waste cloth for bandages. We kept our leeches prepared – half of them plump, gorged with cow's blood, and half of them hungry. We sharpened our knives on the grinding-stone. We oiled the saw-blades for amputations – the small one for fingers and toes, and the large one for limb-bones.

We made our perfume from flower petals and volatile spirit. Brother Fulco and I took twenty trips to the cesspits, collecting the mixed slurry of shit and piss, in our wooden buckets, till we had filled a large cauldron. We kept the vessel outside the infirmary. But Fulco advised we should regularly stick our heads over the edge and avail ourselves of the fumes, and draw in the strong, wholesome vapours, to keep the miasma away and our lungs clean.

For, to fight the plague with our full force, we would need both. The fragrant and the rank. The best of smells and the worst of smells.

'Is that you, Brother Fulco?' I ask.

For the figure that looms before me has Brother Fulco's height and shape. He wears Brother Fulco's feet in Brother Fulco's sandals, attached to his legs, reaching into his robe, with his muscular hands and slender fingers emerging from the sleeves. Only he has a head like a giant crow's, black with a long pointed beak, and two glistening, black, button eyes.

'This will be our protection.' Fulco draws the mask off his pink perspiring head. 'I've made one for each of us. Together with leather gloves and a waxed cape. The miasma will not be able to penetrate. It is my very own invention . . .'

He shows me the inside of the mask, with the dark glass eyes, and the beak packed with straw, mixed with herbs, impregnated with essences.

'I have used rosemary, myrrh, mint, lavender, rose petals and pepper.'

'Yes?'

'It will take a mighty miasma to overpower the scent of all those.'

62

'Indeed, Brother.' His is a clever, wise and ingenious mind. This is a reassurance. Still, even so . . . I have an unease I cannot name.

Between Vespers and Compline, after the lighting of the candles, the mummers perform a drama for our gathered brotherhood. The Abbot has permitted this on the strict promise that the performance should address the sins of Man, offer guidance for redemption, be innocent of any comfort or cheer, and entirely stripped of pleasures.

The leader of the group, who goes by the title of Thomas Jack-Rabbit, or Clever-Legs, or sometimes Johnny-Bare-Arse, comes forth alone to address us. He wears a long coat patched of red and green quadrants. His hose have one yellow leg and one orange. He has one silver shoe and one gold shoe. He doffs his feathered cap and waves it with a flourish.

But when he spins around, and sways from side to side, we see the back of his costume and hose. His reverse is all black, and on it are drawn in white the bones of the human body, topped by a skull, so it seems we are facing a swaying skeleton. When he wiggles his backside, the dead seem to dance.

Then he twists back again, and we see his merry dress, his smiling face and his bulging eyes.

'This is the tale of Life and Death,' he says. 'And it is the oldest story on Earth. And yet man will rarely believe it . . . *Memento mori*,' he says. '*Nous devons mourir* . . . We all must die.

'One day a beautiful lady, a rich merchant and a powerful prince set out on the road together . . .'

Then three more mummers enter from the right, formed in a line, jerking up and down, each riding an invisible horse, their hands reaching forward as if holding the reins. One has long golden hair and wears a long dress. He purses his lips, shakes his long, yellow locks, and winks at us brothers.

The second has a large paunch. The third wears a crown.

Then three more figures appear, coming the other way, all bags of bones with skulls for heads. They carry dripping lumps and tubes, which are parts of their bodies but keep falling out.

And the beautiful lady stops, scowls at the first, and says, 'Why stop me, hag? You are as old as the grave and ugly as sin.'

And the first corpse says, in a low coarse voice, 'I was fresh beauty, fair as a flower, scented as roses. Men fell at my feet. But now the putrid flesh falls off me and I smell of spoiled meat.'

And the merchant turns to the second dead one, and says, 'Why stop me? You are a bag of bones with nothing to sell and no money to buy.'

And the second corpse says, 'Once I was rich like you, stupid and fat as a pig, but you die empty-handed and poor as your soul.'

And the prince turns on the final living corpse, and commands him, 'Be gone. You trespass on my time, and you're blocking my path.'

And the third corpse says, 'Like you, I used to be king of all I surveyed. Then I bit the dust and gave up the ghost. Now all I'm fit for is to be supper for worms.'

'Beauty flees the body,' says the first-dead. 'Time chases it from the face.'

'You can't take your wealth with you,' says the second. 'It belongs in the world.'

'We are all food for the worms,' says the third-dead. 'They go in thin and they come out fat.'

Then the six figures all link arms together, three living and three dead, and begin to swirl in a circle. They dance faster and faster, until they merge to a blurred ring. And the band plays and the music speeds too, led by a Hurdy Gurdy, sounding like a flock of demented bleating sheep.

Thomas Jack-Rabbit steps towards us, the dancers circling behind, until they suddenly all tumble to the ground in a heap.

And Thomas spins around and shows us his skeleton back.

'My name is Death,' he says, 'and I am coming for you. Such as I was, you are. And such as I am you will be. Wealth, beauty and power are lost. The dark door swings open. You cross over to death. The worms are waiting. They are waiting for you.'

Then he clears his throat and commences to sing in a rasping, creaky voice. 'Oh, Death'. We have heard the song before. We know it well.

I am Death, who none can cheat.

I'll snaffle your soul and leave your meat.

I'll clamp your feet so you can't walk.

I'll lock your jaw so you can't talk.

I'll seal your eyes so you can't see.

Feel my chill fingers. Come with me.

I'll rot the flesh from off your frame.

For dirt and worms both have their claim.

Then he sways, wearing a sad, perplexed grin.

Then he releases a quiet, inadvertent gurgling sound, like water leaving a bottle.

Then he topples towards us, hits the floor-stones, full face, with a muffled thud, and lies deadly still.

It is most convincing. And we marvel at his skill in falling so recklessly without care for his cracked head, and acting his own demise so realistically. For truly it is a life-like death.

And the band of musicians fall silent, halted in mid-tune. So we know the show is finished. And we sit still on our benches, waiting for Brother Jack-Rabbit to rise to take our applause. For it is a strong moral, grasped by us all.

Death is abrupt. It comes without warning. It comes for us all.

The three living and the three dead rise from their heap and mutter to each other. They gather around their fallen leader. They tap his cheeks. They loosen his costume. They whisper close in his ears.

Brother Fulco turns to me and pats my wrist. 'Come.

We must help. For, I fear, if Brother Death has not passed already, he is certainly unwell.'

Brother Jack-Rabbit's eyes are closed. His forehead is smeared with blood. His mouth is open. Two of his front teeth have been broken away. He wears a tense grimace of pain.

Brother Fulco lowers his head to the man's chest. Then he draws back an eyelid to reveal a still, bloodshot, staring eye.

'He's still breathing. Fast and shallow. He has a surplus of black bile. His breath smells of brimstone, ale and onion. He is very hot. The sweat on his brow tastes sour and salty.'

Just then, at the edge of my sight, I detect a quick brown blur. And straight away I feel a prickle at my neck.

I know what it is.

A flea has crossed over. It has jumped from the mummer onto me.

It is a bad augury. It is abandoning the sick man. It does not have faith in his future. It wants a safer home. It wants fresh, healthy blood to sup on.

Fulco tears at the man's collar and draws back his shirt to expose his chest. Then we see it, cupped in his arm-pit. It is a blue lump, the size of a crow's egg.

There's no mistaking. It is the swelling that comes with the pox. The dark, weeping lump they name the bubo.

Now, the plague is amongst us.

'May God have mercy on us . . .' Fulco mutters.

The bell rang for Compline, our night's prayers, and the brothers took their place in the line, before wandering in silence to the chapel, not yet knowing what had come amongst them.

But the mummers seemed to know more. They formed a tight huddle, and watched us attend to the sick man. But when I turned their way again, there were fewer there.

I counted. Three of them were gone. And there was heated whispering in the group that remained.

But the next time I turned, there were none.

They all were fled, scattered, sudden as wary starlings, in the blink of an eye, having discarded their costumes, tossed aside, inside out and torn, alongside their abandoned instruments, beside their trampled masks.

They had not even bidden us goodbye, collected their possessions, offered their prayers for a safe journey, said farewell to their poxed comrade, nor thanked us for our hospitality.

We heard the creak of the great door of the monastery opening, the whinny of their pony outside, then the barking of Toby their hound.

'They are fleeing from themselves and hiding from each other,' Brother Fulco said. 'They seek to out-run themselves. And I doubt they will succeed.'

We three infirmarers donned our plague cloaks and masks to handle the man. Now there was a new concern. We had to minimise the chance of pox particles passing through the airs, on the waves of his now thick, sickly aromas, into our own skins.

We came prepared, but the masks muffled our speech, so we were forced to gesture and shout. And the waxed cloaks were heavy, drew a sweat and hampered our work.

We lifted Brother Jack-Rabbit onto a bier and wheeled him to the infirmary.

We laid him on a straw mattress.

He bore a fierce fever. He was racked by coughing. He twisted and contorted with cramps.

We watched more buboes in his groin swell and darken from pink to scarlet, grown from the size of an egg to an apple. Meanwhile, more rose in his arm-pits and on his neck.

He tossed in some delirium, shouting, whispering and hissing. Though we could not grasp the full sense in it, we could make out some coarse, rude phrases.

He took to vomiting small puddles of black blood, and sneezing red blood in a hazy spray.

'You must repent your sins,' Fulco leaned over to advise. 'Before you leave us.'

The man twitched the closed lids of his eyes and ground his teeth together. But he had nothing to say.

By dawn his body had slowed and his appearance had worsened. The tips of his toes and fingers, his lips and nose darkened from purple to black.

'His flesh is dying,' said Fulco, 'from the inside out.'

The man's breath came noisy, forced and fast as though it was a mighty struggle. There was an awkward, unhelpful gurgling sound from his throat, as if he was trying to gargle his spittle.

'That is the sound of the soul,' said Fulco. 'It is growing restless. It is looking for the best way out of the prison of his body.'

'The soul leaves through the throat?'

'There are nine gateways – the two eyes, the two ears, the two nostrils, the mouth and . . .' He paused and coughed apologetically. 'Sometimes through the organs of excretion, the penis or the anus.'

'Yes?'

'Sometimes the soul sounds the trumpet of the bowels as it parts through the back door. Or it trickles out with a final piss. It doesn't stand on ceremony or plead its dignity. It just wants to be free of the prison of flesh. It just seeks its immortality.'

When the man finally parted this world, it was at Prime, the early morning prayers, as we heard our brothers chant '*Salva Mira Creatura*' distantly in the chapel.

Brother Jack-Rabbit's soul chose to part Brother Jack-Rabbit's body through his nose, in a long final sneeze, spraying blood and snot in a hazy ball around his head. Then his head snapped to the side. His chest jerked. Then he breathed no more.

We felt a rush of wind and a cold breeze brush our faces.

'Did you feel that?' Fulco asked.

'Yes.'

'That was his spirit rushing out,' said Fulco. 'Sometimes they linger for hours. But this one is in a hurry to be gone.'

'I have never seen a dead man before,' I told Fulco, 'not up close.'

'That's not a man. It is an empty shell of him. Now the spirit has gone out.'

Fulco was right. The face was waxy and stiff. It looked nothing like the man who had been alive. It looked like a crude mask. There was no life or emotion to the face, except, perhaps, a look of mild surprise.

All of a sudden, I felt dog-tired.

I was in the burning grip of some fever.

Trickles of sweat ran down my cheeks.

There was a hammering in my skull, making me wince at every blow.

I took myself to my new cell in the corridor off the infirmary.

I laid myself down and the dark took me.

VIII. God Only Knows

I cannot tell how much time has passed.

There is a hammering on the closed oak door of my cell.

'Who is there?' I call between the thunderous blows. I would rise to answer, but my aching legs refuse the call. I'm held down in my bed by a fierce grip.

'It is us . . . Brother Fulco and Brother James.'

'Come in,' I call, 'no need to knock.'

The knocking stops, but the door stays firmly closed.

'We do not need to come in, Brother,' James calls out.

'Never mind,' Fulco calls, 'it's better we stay outside.'

'What are you doing?'

'We are securing your door,' says Fulco.

'*Securing?*'

'Closing. With a plank and some nails,' says James.

'But I'm still inside.'

'Yes, Brother, we know . . . But it is safer this way. So we keep apart. Sealed by the door.'

'Why so?'

There is a long silence before Fulco answers. 'Because you carry the plague, Brother Diggory.'

'Yes . . .' I say.

I guessed as much, from the hammering in my skull, the leaden weight of my body, the trickles of sweat down my face, the lumps – hard as acorns – that my fingers feel on my neck and in the pits of my arms.

'This pestilence,' says Fulco, 'it is everywhere. It has spread amongst us like wild-fire. So many brothers have fallen to its clutch. We must separate the sick – like you – from the healthy. Now segregation is our last defence.'

'May God be with you,' James calls. 'He loves you so well. As we all do.'

'You are always in our prayers,' Fulco says. 'Always. We pray God preserves you.'

'What shall I eat?'

There is a brief silence, until Brother James replies.

'Trust to the Lord. He always provides.'

'But best think of your immortal soul,' suggests Fulco, 'which matters more.'

I must have fallen again into a demented, fevered sleep. In the cauldron of the illness, with my flesh burning, I dreamed I was in Hell's Fire.

In my dream, this is the way of Hell –

i. Thousands of demented souls, as numerous as the stalks in a field of wheat, are all screaming without pause.

ii. The sinners are suspended by hooks through their bellies above an orange cauldron. You smell your own flesh roasting. And feel the burn of your scorching fat.

iii. Demons with the heads of snakes and lizards come sup upon you, tearing the flesh from you.

iv. Then the flesh grows back so you may be gobbled again.

When I wake, I find myself panting like an exhausted dog. I believe my own howling woke me. I am curled up in a ball, like an unborn. And sucking my thumb. The dark shadow of a visitor is cast over my body.

It is a tall, thin man, perhaps six foot-lengths in height. He is stooped over my cot. His head is sunk in the dark depths of a baggy hood. He wears a thick black habit reaching to his feet, so I guess he is a Benedictine brother. He has come straight from harvesting – for he has brought his scythe with him, laid close by his feet.

I sniff the foul, tainted air.

'What's that smell?' I ask.

'Smell?' His deep, croaking voice sounds hurt, taken aback. 'What smell?'

'It is rotten meat, and fusty mildew, and shit. All rolled up together.'

'Is it me?' He sounds hurt but resigned.

'Forgive me,' I say, 'I meant no offence.'

'People do say I carry a certain smell,' he concedes, 'but I do not have the nose to tell . . .'

When he turns to regard me, I see a white, hollow-cheeked, tight-lipped face, the skin drawn taut across the skull. His gums have receded into his lipless jaw, so he displays a fine set of long, horsey teeth.

His black eyes carry silvery clusters of speckled stars, as if the whole night sky rotates within the orbits of his head.

It is not clear if he is smiling, scowling, or grimacing in some private pain.

He makes a clanking noise when he gestures. It is like the dull clatter of bone on bone.

'Are you a stranger to these parts?' I ask.

'I come. I go . . . I am here. I am there . . . I am everywhere . . .' He sounds weary with his lot.

'You meet many people?' I say. 'In your travels?'

'I meet everyone in time,' he concedes, 'but just the once.'

'I suppose you are well known, then?'

'I am famous. My craft is legend. And my work is never done.'

'Is there not a quiet season for your trade?'

'Autumn drops the leaves. Winter blows chill winds. In spring many shoots don't sprout. In summer fresh fruit always tumbles from the bough.'

'You've come here to see *me*?'

'I have,' he says. 'For, in time, I must call on everyone . . .'

'There's some mistake? You're surely looking for someone else?'

'No. I am come just for you.'

He sniffs and looks away. There is a long rattling sigh of bone resonating on bone.

'I never expect a welcome.' He splays his arms. He shakes his hooded head. He shows his empty palms and long bony fingers. 'I come unasked, for the truly ungrateful. Everyone blames the messenger. I get no thanks . . . Most plead for more time. As if it's mine to gift . . .'

'They do?'

'Bold men draw their swords to fight me. Cowards hide under the table. Fools pretend not to know me. Women offer me the bribe of love, saying they will lie in my grasp, if only they can rise again after. The rich try to gift me money. The poor beg, or offer up their soggy crusts.'

'Yes?'

'Or they plead they're the wrong person, and I should take their neighbour instead.'

'Yes?'

'Enough,' he snaps. 'Come . . . your hourglass has emptied. All the sand has run out . . . We have to move on.'

Then I hear my soul's slithering, gurgling departure. It is the last sound of my body.

I go out moistly, through my throat, with a long croaking sound, like an indignant toad.

I lift up, weightless, to the rafters. I ride the air like a gull. I look down to my still body, the mouth splayed open in a stupid smile, the tongue poking out to the side, my open eyes gazing blankly up.

I am calm. My thoughts are clear.

Now I am dead, I feel more alive than ever before.

Now I am free of that bony brain-box with its tufted top, that awkward lumpy jacket of flesh, those clumsy, gawky limbs, those troublesome holes, venting those messy tubes, always sucking something in and squeezing some other stuff out.

Time is gone. Colours are brighter. All is serene. There's a bright light beckoning.

And I see the journey of my life, from birth to death,

played out in its entirety, with every movement and thought and feeling, every sight and sound and smell and touch. It lasts forever, and yet it comes and goes in the blink of an eye.

Then beneath comes a billowing darkness, a thick smoky blackness, and I know this is the worst there was, could ever be, a separateness, an isolation, an interminable loneliness. Foul nothing. Without end.

And the smoke draws around me, and I realise if it swallows me I shall be lost, gone for all eternity with no hope.

And I realise there are other lost souls about me, but they too are wrapped in their own fog and unable to reach out and make any contact. So all I know is their presence, and the impossibility of any connection. That no one here can ever touch anyone else. For we are all lost. And will be for all eternity.

And I scream it out –

'God forgive me. God spare me.'

Then suddenly I lift up, angling off to the left. Now, I'm jostled by things friendly, but I can't tell by what, by whom. There's a hazy greyness, stretching into a tube, brightening as I rise. Incandescent specks are drifting past, some fast, some slower, like specks of dust, dancing in a sun-beam. And I understand. We're all family together, all souls on our journeys, drifting our individual paths. The sides of the tunnel come clearer, silvery. The light at the end is glowing golden, brighter and close.

The light beckons, inviting. This light loves me. It understands everything. It forgives all.

I need to bathe in that light, like I've never needed before.

There's the grumble of distant thunder, then an explosion of light rolling out all around me. Its golden joy shines brighter than the sun. But it doesn't dazzle the eyes. I am at the centre of the light, which shines entirely for me.

I am the love of the world.

My past, my present, my future have come together, layered in fluorescent skeins around me. Now I see my life, in all directions, all times. I see how the smallest happenings piece together to make the whole. The bee-sting, the curdled milk, the grazed knee, the pig-squeal and the fallen leaf are all inevitable and connected. None can happen without the other. There's no guilt or regret, just how you judge yourself.

'I am the light,' the radiance tells me. 'I am the Love Eternal.'

'And I am Brother Diggory,' I tell him, 'from the Order of Odo at Whye. Carried off by the plague. Perhaps you've been expecting me?'

Go forth, angel.

Now, it doesn't voice itself, the light. Instead, it *shows* profound. It leaks this luminous, radiant music, of a harp sounding heart-strings, and a horn blown by kindness, scented with camomile, rosemary and sage, resonating into shimmering waves of truth that dance into the spaces, filling the gaps in your mind with joy.

'We live to love.' I know it now. 'We must only love.'

Then there's the gorgeous riff, of seven luminous chords, telling me all there is to be known, about Our Lord, our life, our purpose. It's utterly simple, extraordinarily strange, and unspeakably beautiful.

'God's truth?' I gasp. 'And I never knew.'

'Man never knows,' the light confides, 'until he sheds his blinkered body.'

'I can't wait to tell them all. Those down below,' I say.

Dear Lord, Blessed Jesus, you know that feeling? When you've said something terribly wrong? Or out of place? And there's no way you can unsay it, or make amends?

It's even worse when you're addressing the Almighty, King of Kings, the Light of the Ages.

The light leaps back. The radiance dims. There's a chill wind with icy spits of rain.

'You are come too early,' the light murmurs, and wanes. 'You are still attached to your heart and sinews.'

'Can I not stay?' I plead. 'After I've come so far?'

But the gloom and the cold are unrelenting.

'Can I keep the truth? And take it back down to Earth?'

Then, there's an almighty clack and a dismal whirr. It's the seven chords played backwards, harsh as finger-nails scraping slate tiles, crushed hopes, howling babies, splintering bones.

And suddenly it's dark, and I'm tugged downwards, like scum through a cold, slimed piping.

The tube is sucking me deeper, darker.

I hear a foul, sniffy, slurpy sound.

Shhlooooop . . .

That's my spirit, returning. Going back the way it came, snuffled up my nose, then down my throat, like a lump of gory phlegm.

Time returns. Worry follows. Pain comes close behind. Colours are dull and tarnished now. The air stinks of piss, must and rot.

Yes, I'm back in my awful, aching, needy body, shivering with cold, my teeth chattering.

I lie day upon day upon day – four or five, I cannot be sure – writhing on my cot, sometimes roasting, sometimes frozen, far too weak to rise, but just too strong to die.

When I next wake, my mind seems clearer, my body stronger.

My eyes are drawn to a scurrying shape. I spy it from the corner of my little eye. A small brown furry thing is moving across the floor of my cell. It jerks forward then stops, raises its whiskered snout to sniff the air, then scampers forwards, then stops again. There is some object on the floor before it.

It twists its head. Its popping black berry eyes regard me. Its whiskers twitch. It opens its mouth. To disclose its yellow teeth.

It is a small brown rat. And it is trying to carry off my candle, which is too large to clutch in its jaws. So Brother Rat is trying to roll it across the floor, pushing with its snout, then prodding it on with its front paws.

And I wonder what good Christian use a rat could find for a candle. Being a beast and an unbeliever, without need of the redemptive symbolism of a shining light, and well able to see unaided in that dismal gloom we humans call the dark.

Then I see the tooth-marks along the length. Then I realise.

Of course.

The candle is made of rendered mutton fat.

It is food.

It is fine, greasy, sustaining food.

Then I understand too. That I am being robbed. I am being robbed of what I most need.

Robbed by a rat, attempting to carry off the only food I have left in my cell.

And yet I thank the Lord, who has provided in this time of need. Who has shown me, through the admirable example of this small, industrious, thieving creature, how I might secure the means to sustain myself.

He always provides.

'Scat,' I say, with all the clamour and menace I can summon.

Brother Rat looks to me, then looks down to the candle before him. He pauses. He twitches his whiskers. Then he starts to roll it again. But more hurriedly now. He is headed for the narrow gap beneath the wooden door of my cell.

So now the race is on. Between two impeded contestants. A monk disabled by the plague, and a rat labouring to roll a candle many times his bulk.

I can take little pride in emerging as winner. It was an

uneven contest. For the Almighty has already favoured me with every advantage – superior bulk, a cleverer mind, and an immortal soul to weigh the moralities.

But I am panting from the efforts of moving two paces from my bed, then reaching down to grasp the candle.

Brother Rat emits a high-pitched squeak of distress as I pull the candle up and away.

I slump backwards onto my bed. I do not pause, for Grace or anything. No, I straightaway commence to gnaw upon the lower, stubbier end of the candle.

Although it is crumbly and dry upon the palate, it is a greatly satisfying waxiness with its unctuous richness and smoky, gamey flavours. I believe I have never enjoyed a candle so completely, before or since.

Brother Rat releases a pitiful squeal. I see him watching me intently, grieving his loss, perched upon his back legs, with his front paws raised, as if in prayer, with his pink tongue lolling.

So I relent. I take a thick flake of candle and toss it down to him.

As he helped me, so I help him. For we are kin – brothers in misfortune, both struggling to survive.

He looks to me. Then he looks to the morsel. Then he hesitantly trots forward, sniffs my scent upon it, before he lifts it up to claim it between his grasping front paws.

Soon we are munching in unison, in hungry harmony.

I chew off more than I can swallow, scattering more pieces his way.

It is then, I believe, that our true friendship forms.

I call him *Frater Rattus*, in the Latin manner. And within days he learns to answer to that name, and comes when I call him. And perches on my shoulder. And rides in my pocket. And will submit to having his back stroked and his cheeks rubbed, and his whiskers tickled.

And so I baptise him.

Partly as amusement and partly so I should have another Christian for companion. Whatever the moral shortcomings of a rat's soul. For, as you shall hear shortly, I will be in need of any company I might find.

And I call him my Franciscan brother, because he too is a comrade of the animals, a dirt-poor beggar, and, like the followers of Saint Francis, he wears the coarse coat of shabby brown.

IX. The Cure for Life

As I lay in my filthy cassock in my sweat-sodden bedding, smelling the warm ferment of my juices, I become aware of the frisky motions of my fleas making free with my steamy flesh, hopping here and there, wherever I took their fancy, then nipping me hard. Perhaps, in my inactive state abed, I had become an easy target, an invitation to a feast, so had gathered more fleas than my fair share.

It was Brother Fulco's opinion that fleas were given to mankind at Creation. So Adam had them. And even Eve. It was Fulco's further observation that a monk of average size and customary cleanliness was likely host to four or five fleas. But we should not presume to call them our own. For they were a gift of God, besides being mobile, fickle in their affections, and, like mosquitoes, would move from brother to brother, favouring the sanguine more than the bilious for the savour of their blood. Or simply preferred a change of home and varied diet.

Scholars are fiercely divided on the moral character of the flea.

We know Saint Francis of Assisi called them the pearls of the poor, and said the more you hosted, the holier you were. He observed they were ornaments to wear upon our skin, God's gift to us, and argued they depicted the Ladder of Creation, how we were all animals of the Lord,

85

dependent on each other to live and let live. So, if we eat meat ourselves, we should not begrudge the flea some small supper of us.

But James of Rochester had a sterner judgement, claiming that the flea was amongst the cruellest and fiercest of beasts. Hence its scale. For he said that the Lord had given the animals their size in proportion to their mildness of character. Thus the whale and elephant were allowed their largeness because they were gentle and kindly beasts, unless roused by attack. And that if the flea was built to the same proportion it would be the worst monster of Creation, for its sole ambition was murder, and would leave in its wake a trail of bloodless corpses, with all the humanity sucked out of them, just dry, empty husks of skin. So to temper the flea's malignant nature, God had made it very small.

I had noticed, these last few days, how the monastery had fallen quiet. There was no sound of movement in the passage past my cell, no noise or talk from the infirmary, no distant chant or plainsong from the chapel, no calls of the brothers at work, no summoning the animals in for their fodder, no ringing of the bell calling the brothers to prayer.

All I heard were the beasts. The snorting swine, rooting close by the wall. The forlorn bellowing of our cows, as if still waiting to be milked, tormented by their low swinging udders. The crowing of the cockerel. The night howls of the vixen. The mockery of the cuckoo. The hoot of the owl. Lost souls rustling the leaves.

I knew I was growing stronger – that by some miracle, and gift of God, I had suffered the plague and survived, which none thought was possible.

I garnered from this miraculous survival that I was special. Perhaps that I had been saved by my innocence and my goodness, though I was not sure, since babes and saints had perished. Or that I had simply arrived in eternity too early. Or, more likely, that the Lord had saved me to fulfil some purpose, such as he had spoken to me when I visited him briefly in Heaven, but which conversation I had – regrettably – forgotten. But which, I prayed, would return to my memory in the fullness of time. I could stand now on my own two legs, with near steadiness. But I was parched as the desert and knew I must find release and water.

I commence to shout for help.

'Brother Fulco . . .' I call. 'Brother James . . .'

The birds fall silent briefly. A goat bleats at a distance. But no man answers.

'Brother *anyone* . . .'

I strike the door with my palm, then hammer it with a fist, but there is just a dull unrelenting thud with no resonant give to it.

'Let me out,' I cry.

I kick low down at the cross-piece. I barge the door with a shoulder, and hear a sharp splintering and sense a rumour of movement. The door gives to a finger's width. I heave again and again with my shoulder until, at the fifth collision, the door gives a tearing, splintering sound and swings wide open.

I want the outdoors. I am stumbling down the passageway to the door to the monastery garden. I dunk my head in the water barrel through the surface film and swallow down the brackish water. The frog-spawn, green slime and water-snails must mind for themselves.

I drink down a bucketful. I raise my head from the barrel. I shake the water from my head. I sit on the stone wall of the garden and calm my heaving breath and thumping chest. I close my eyes and join my hands.

> Angel of God, my guardian dear,
> to whom God's love commits me here,
> ever this day be at my side,
> to light and guard, to rule and guide.
> Amen.

There are no brothers to be seen, no smoke from the kitchen chimney, no prayer bells, no chant from the chapel, no clatter of wooden buckets from the dairy, no chopping of wood, no calls to the beasts.

I fear things are bad.

But I find them worse.

When I return to the sanatorium, I find my brothers Fulco and James there at their stations.

Fulco sits bolt upright in his chair by the dead grey ashes of the fire. In his lap rests the hide-bound tome *Tacuinum*

Sanitatis by Ibn Butlan of Baghdad, in the Latin translation. It is open at the section on the seven sure cures for plagues, scourges and pestilences. My brother's red-veined eyes look upwards to the heavens. His gaze is tired and discouraged. He is very still, and there is no pulse from his cold wrist. His curled talon-fingers are blackened at the tips. His soul has long since left its lodgings.

Brother James is there in body, too, yet departed in spirit, sprawled upon the slate paving, his head splayed sideways, as if trying to watch his back. His fingers and nose are purpled with rot.

Brothers Andrew, Franklin and Mark lie in the cots down the sanatorium wall, contorted tangled limbs, as if the pox has tied the string of them into clumsy knots.

Many flies, bluebottles and wasps have come to keep them company. And they sound a happy, busy, harmonious buzzing, as their small battalions swarm across their faces and exposed skin.

The smells of it all are warm, rich, putrid and pungent. The air stings my eyes, burns in my nose and scorches my lungs.

I retreat once more to the herb garden.

A long deep grave has been dug, perhaps ten paces by eight. The area and depth of the excavation shows that the digger was expecting a large harvest of cadavers, to be buried in haste, on top of each other.

At the base of the pit, two bodies show under a scatter of earth. Only their feet protrude. I believe I recognise the sandals of Brother Michael and the cow-herd's boots of

Brother Aubrey splayed to his flat-footed gait.

In the chapel, the Abbot is sprawled sideways in the pulpit, sunk to his knees. His eyes are closed in prayer.

He was addressing fifteen brothers, spread wide apart on the benches, as if afraid to be close to each other, or lacking common feeling, who then chose the occasion to rest there, in prayer and chant, until death chose another place for them.

I did what I could. I paid all the respect I should. But I am not a large or strong man, and it is tiring work dragging a large stiff corpse by the feet and lifting it onto a bier.

The labour was made harder still, for the sickness had taken its toll of me. I had become scrawny and bony-ribbed. I still had intermittent fever with blinding headaches.

Small lumps came and went in my groin, as if some remnant of the pox.

My skin carried the sulphurous taint of the rot.

While I had suffered and defeated the pestilence, still it somehow clung to my side.

So I saw in thirty-odd forms how this pestilence used a human being, and ate it away from the inside out, a blue rot reaching through like the veins of a cheese, till it erupted in purpled bubbles on the skin, and squirted out the life-blood in black clots from the mouth and nose, and tied the body in tangled knots, and contorted the faces in gurning grimaces of pain, and turned warm, live, loving flesh into cold rancid meat, and gave off its sick, sweet stenches of putrescence, shit, decayed eggs and rotted teeth.

It took me the best part of two days of sweaty, limb-deadening, back-aching work to carry all my brothers to their final resting place. I thanked the Lord someone else had had the foresight of catastrophe, and dug such a monstrous large hole in advance of my need.

At first I buried my brothers by the place of their death. Emptying first the sanatorium, then the chapel.

I felt forlorn, lonely and melancholy, and was many times moved to hot, heavy tears. I felt myself poorly used by my fates, to lose so many friends and family all together. Yet I saw that, since I was still alive, my fortune was better than theirs.

Then, fearing that the communal grave would be full before all the dead were housed, in which case I should need to dig another hole, I sought to arrange them by a pattern, to a principle of best fit.

In this, I remembered Fulco's lessons, and took Pythagoras of Samos as my guide, in his theorem of the triangle, as proved by Euclid.

$$(a \times a) + (b \times b) = c \times c$$

where a is the height of the middlemost brother, b the measure of the little-most, and c the length of the tallest, otherwise known as Brother Hypotenuse

This way, I laid them out on the grass, in triplets of ascending size – tall, medium, short – and moved them to and fro, and spun some around, and in my mind's eye imagined the different shapes their triangulations might make together. For there is an economy of space in laying one's loved ones head to foot to head to foot to head, with two or three bellies centremost, especially as some are fat, and all are set so stiff.

Between each layer of brothers I scattered a thin cover of soil. This way, each had his own grave, yet had the comfort of the close proximity of his own kind, his fondest friends.

So frugal was I of the space, and so ingenious at fitting all those very different shapes and sizes together, that at the end, when I had buried thirty-two brothers, there was still ample space left in the north-west corner of the pit.

I knew I should keep the Abbot's ring, chain and crucifix. For these belonged not to him or his dead body, but to the living Order of Odo, which now consisted of . . . me alone.

I tried tugging the gold and emerald band from his fat finger – with the help of duck fat from the larder – but the band was too narrow on his plump sausage finger that I was required to seek the cutting advice of a knife. Then a thought came to me of great significance and clarity. And that concerned me most particularly.

In the long history of the Order of Odo, whenever death fashioned a vacancy, the Abbot was selected by his brothers as the individual of highest spiritual merit whose example they could respect, and whose authority they could thus accept.

Of the thirty-nine brothers of the order, thirty-two were slain by the plague, dead and buried. Six were missing, presumed dead, or fled from their sacred vocation. Only one monk remained within the order, to carry the tradition and take on authority as leader of the community and bearer of the faith.

Thus, I eased the ring upon my finger, and acknowledged myself as the new Abbot of the Order of Odo, of the monastery at Whye, not because I was vainglorious or ambitious for personal advancement, but because it was my solemn duty, having been selected by circumstances of God's devising, and appointed without any dissenting voice by all the surviving monks, which were myself.

Thus, to observe the due formalities, I said a short service, in order that I might bless myself, and placed the Abbot's cap upon my head, so elevating myself. I returned my original name to myself, declaring that henceforth I should be known as Brother Jack Fox, Abbot of Whye.

I addressed a few words, to history and myself.

I swore to do my utmost for the Order of Saint Odo. I prayed for God's aid, and the support of His angels.

No sooner was I elected Abbot – by the will of God and assent of Man – than the Lord moved me. I began to assume the eyes and mind of authority, and plan for the future well-being of our monastery.

If the Order of Odo was to survive, it would need to gain new members in a time to come, when the plague was abated and fears quelled. Until that time, I should need to preserve the heritage and the items of utmost value from the hands of jackals, thieves and passing wastrels, and from the depredations of time and weather.

Amongst these valuables I counted – the reliquary boxes containing the skull-bones of our founder, Saint Odo; the written works of Saint Odo, being *The Book of Life* and *The Great Unhappened*, and all copies of these; the silver altar furniture, including the crucifix, the pyx and paten; the ciborium, together with the painted triptych of Our Lord Jesus; the Great Bible of Whye; the funds in gold and silver coinage held in the Abbot's chest.

With all these, the order could build itself again, on the foundations of its past. Without these, it was lost.

I was mindful, too, that I should need money and valuables to fund the re-establishment of the monastery and support the chapter of monks, however many it should come to be, though currently it numbered only me.

But, realising I was to be the root of this tree, I recognised I must be well nourished, if only for the sake of posterity.

To these ends, I resolved to keep in my possession a few gold groats, the Abbot's ring and crucifix, the pyx, the skull-bones of Odo, and the original copy of *The Book of Life* – they being too valuable to leave unattended.

Then I thought where to consign the valuables I should leave behind, but worried myself that wherever they were hidden or dug under, they would risk discovery, from the signs of dislodged stones or moved earth.

So I thought to hide them in plain sight, where the world could see a burial, but where none would choose to dig it up.

I placed it all in the plague-blasted grave of the rotting brothers.

The reliquary box went in a larger wooden chest. The coins and silver went in an iron cauldron from the kitchen, which I sealed over with a layer of molten wax. The books I wrapped in parcels of oiled hide, to preserve them from the damp.

I trusted that no one would have the ill, insanitary sense to dig up a mass grave of plague-poxed monks.

I knew I must leave the monastery.

It was a dirtied, sick place, blighted by plague.

Everyone would skirt by, except thieves come to plunder.

The place must be cleansed by abandonment and time.

In a year, maybe two, it would be fit to return.

I considered my appearance. I did not want to go forth locally as a brother from the monastery, for those around would know the plague had reached us and would fear I carried the contagion.

So I shaved my head, to lose the tonsured ring, so I'd appear a monk no more. And I found a thick blanket-cloak, and russet wool tunic and hose knotted with rope. I thought I should pass as shoddy, as a poor man, to give no suggestion of the hidden wealth I carried, and to attract less interest or concern.

Imagine my sorrow when I reached into the pocket of my tunic and felt an oddly still, stiff, cold parcel of fur.

I pulled it out and laid it down on a paving-stone.

It was Brother Rattus, eyes open, glazed and opaque,

with an expression of bewilderment, his limbs stretched out stiff, like the legs of a refectory stool. His underside was pocked with small swellings, dark as blackberries. The only movement was from the flea that leapt out from his belly fur, onto the cuff of my tunic.

Yes, Brother Rattus, too, had died of the plague.

My sole remaining friend was gone without warning. I had never felt so alone or abandoned.

The pox had taken every body I loved.

I decided I would set out in the early light, with the sack of my valuables slung over my shoulder. The Lord had spared me from the plague. I believed myself charmed, protected, that He had a higher purpose for me. As I planned my journey, I anticipated trials and tests and tribulations. Yet I had no idea that the world should be so very wicked in the ways it proved. For, on this hard road I trod, I was to meet all manner of challenges from unbelievers, hypocrites, liars, blasphemers, drunks, cheats, thieves, fornicators, and men possessed of unclean minds, ugly dreams, ill will, bad faith, foul tempers, violent manners and deceitful ways as, all the while, the Black Pox dogged my steps.

X. Into the Woods

I walk out early in the crisp, morning air. I trust God to lead me safely.

> Dear Lord, hear this sorry sinner's prayer.
> Protect me from the foul pestilence that stalks in the
>   darkness,
> And from the wolves and ruffians that lurk in the
>   shadows.
> And may I find good fortune and kind companions,
> And, God willing, encounter woman too.

I find cheer on my new path, even if I am not yet fully recovered. I still have bouts of fever and the sweat flows in rivulets down my cheeks. Small lumps sprout in my neck or groin, then shortly disappear.

It is as if I am suffering from memory of the pestilence, reviving its symptoms in miniature.

A monk may move slower than a Godless soul, for he must observe the Liturgy of the Hours, pausing to say his prayers, seven times a day.

There is much to be said, and much to be prayed for. There is Matins at mid-night, Lauds at dawn, Terce mid-morning, Sext at mid-day, None mid-afternoon, Vespers in the evening, and Compline at night.

The world is a wicked enough place already, and if those in holy orders did not pray so often, it would find itself still worse.

So it is, I am observing the obligations of my calling, in an acorn-strewn clearing in the Forest of Whye, with the sun flickering through the dancing canopy of leaves overhead, as I kneel, knees damp, eyes closed, my arms resting on the trunk of a fallen oak.

I am aware of the love of God, and His Majesty in the wonders of Creation. Then I become aware of something else besides.

There begins a melodic whistling behind me, that sounds human, not birdly nor beastly. So I rise and turn with a start.

There he is. A man sits no more than six paces behind me. He is a scrawny, short man with an incessant twitch to his left cheek, neat, wavy red hair, parted over a broad forehead. His steady gaze engages me, with its strange aspect. For the right eye is the palest blue, while the left is dark brown. He has a dark woollen jacket with broad brass buttons. I observe that he has lost his left ear, somewhere along life's path, as if it has been sheared clean off with a sharp blade.

He is seated, cross-legged, whittling the end of a long staff with a knife. He does this one-handed, holding the stick firm between his knees. His right arm is a stump. Sometime, somehow he's managed to lose his hand, lopped off just above the wrist.

His left cheek twitches, tugging at the side of his

mouth. He wears a reluctant smile, as if he were being tickled against his will.

'You must be careful hereabouts,' he advises.

'Yes?'

'It's a dangerous place. There are desperate people about. Thieves, murderers, poachers, outlaws, heretics.'

'Yes?'

'So you must not turn your back on the world, as you did just now. Or disregard one-footed people, such as me, hopping along in your wake for miles, hoping to attract your kind notice.'

'Thanks,' I say, 'for the advice.'

'Some men would mash your head in with a club. Or cut your throat.'

'They would?'

'Just to have your fine, thick cloak. But mostly to steal whatever you carry in that fat sack, there.'

'Oh,' I concede.

'Never mind me,' he says. 'Finish whatever you have to do, there on your knees. With whoever you are talking to.'

'As it happens,' I say, 'I must move on.'

'You must?'

'At once,' I explain. 'I am already late.'

'Have no care for me,' he shrugs. 'If I wanted to harm you, you'd already be hurt.'

Then he asks me if I was praying, and if so, what for.

I say yes, that I want to repent of many mortal sins.

He asks, 'What sins are those?'

99

I say, 'Gluttony. Pride. Avarice. Sloth. Covetousness. Heresy. Idolatry . . .'

'Yes?' He looks at me hard, unblinking, and crinkles his brow.

'And murder . . .' I improvise. I guess it would do no harm to warn him that I am a desperate and dangerous man.

'Murder?'

'And perjury . . .' I go on. 'Adultery and many fornications.'

'Fornications, you say?' His one ear swivels in interest.

'Of many forms,' I explain, 'involving unnatural postures, repetition, with lustful looking, on the Lord's Day, in broad daylight, and at night with candles, with spilling, and with kissing. With and without fondling and fingers . . .'

'So . . .' He whistles quietly and shakes his head in awe of my achievements. 'For a young man you have made yourself busy.'

'Well,' I explain, 'I have not done every last one of these yet. But I surely intend to.'

'Yes?'

'And then I will repent.'

'You will?'

'With all my heart.'

'And what then?' he enquires.

'Then Christ will forgive me,' I say.

'He will?'

'Oh, yes. For Our Saviour loves no one so much as the repentant sinner. As we know from the Gospel of Luke, and the Parable of the Prodigal Son. For he was lost but then was found.'

'Then you are sinning first, to repent later?'

'Exactly so,' I say. 'For now I have nothing to repent, nothing to offer. I have not lived. I have no virtue, for I have never been tested by temptation. I cannot be good until I have been sinful. Then turned away from evil.'

'If you want to sin,' he says, 'if you sincerely want to sin, and to sin seriously and sin often . . .' He pauses. He frowns. He is carefully planning his words.

'Yes?' I enquire.

'You could do worse than keep me company. I don't know every last mortal sin that the Church has devised to condemn us for trying, but I have practised most of the popular ones, and some unlikely ones besides . . . I can set you on your way, at least.'

I consider this in silence. I doubt how much he might teach me, and whether he is as conversant with so many sins as he brags.

He asks me my name.

I tell him my name is Jack Fox.

I do not reveal that I have recently been elevated to become the Most Reverend Abbot of the Order of Odo, from the monastery at Whye. For I neither want to alert him to my wealth, nor present myself vainly as his better, and unsettle him from his evident ease.

He says his name is Simon Mostly.

I observe that this sounds a fine, unusual name, and ask if Mostly was the village of his birth.

101

No, he says. His acquaintances call him that because, over the years, he has been harshly whittled down by life. Yet, although he has lost an ear in a brawl, been taxed a hand by a vengeful squire, and had left his right foot snapped off in a steel man-trap, and so is several parts less than he has been, still he remains *mostly* himself.

Then he turns his curiosity back to me. He enquires what I bear in my sack.

I make no mention of the crucifix and pyx of silver, the master copy of *The Book of Life*, and the bones of Saint Odo. I simply say I carry some small belongings and some food.

He remarks that he is pleased to hear of the food. He says a man grows tired of snails and slugs, leaves and lichen, gut-ache and hunger.

'There's not much,' I explain, 'just some cheese. Some boiled duck eggs. Some smoked sausage. Some dried fruit. Some salted fish.'

'Yes.' His eyes swivel and sparkle. 'That would suit me well. Thank you for sharing . . .'

Perhaps I sense a threat. For I close my eyes in momentary prayer. A psalm comes to mind.

> Lord, rescue me from evil people;
> protect me from cruel people
> who make evil plans, who always start fights.

But I have no clear recollection what happens next. For oblivion grabs me there and then, and squeezes me hard in its tight black fist. Then holds me there for many hours.

*

When I woke the sun was low. There was a storm breaking in my head with dazzling flashes of lightning and deafening claps of thunder. It felt as though an eager stonemason was chiselling my forehead from the inside.

I felt a thick crust of dried blood on my temple, flaking off like rust.

Looking to my side, I saw that Simon Mostly was gone. And a thief had made himself free with my bag and its contents.

The sack itself lay flat, open-necked and empty on the ground.

It seemed that all my food was missing, although I saw fragments of egg-shell, duck-blue, and a discarded herring tail, and some silvery fish-scales, lying alongside a cheese-rind.

The crucifix and the pyx were gone, but both the skulls of Saint Odo remained, resting calmly on the mossy earth, turned to face me, the eye-sockets staring vacant, pondering life's unresolvable riddle, but with the teeth smiling broadly my way.

The Book of Life was mostly reduced to flaky ashes. Its pages had been torn out and used to feed the flames of a fire. Only the charred binding of the book remained, together with seven pages detailing the Pygmy People of Sicily. So, as a work of universal reference, its use was lost.

Simon Mostly was nowhere to be seen.

I saw his retreating, hopping footstep in the soft earth and trampled leaves.

He was gone.

After feeling the lump on my scalp, and the crust of blood flaking to the touch, and surveying the reduced belongings laid before me, I concluded I had been hit upon the head with a club, then robbed.

I was not slow to heed this as a warning, and as a caution for the days to come.

I must be less trusting. Clearly, not all men in the wider world behaved with the gentle manners of holy brothers in a monastery.

At least I still retained my six gold coins and Abbot's ring, which I had taken care to stow in a lamb's leather drawstring purse, in a dark recess, a private place where a stranger to my person would need be unnaturally curious to look.

> Steal not that book, Mostly, friend,
> in fear damnation be your end.
> For if they burn you to a cinder,
> it'll be for taking truth as tinder.

XI. I Chance upon Woman
and Find Her Good

We do not yet know how the angels talk to each other, whether in Latin, Aramaic, Greek, or some Angelic tongue all their own. Or if they simply know each other's thoughts, even without speaking. For the Bible neglects to tell us which. But it does reveal some shapes and sizes of angels, and their works and places in Heaven and Earth.

In the first sphere of Heaven, around the throne of God, the Son Incarnate, are the fiery Seraphim, too dazzling to gaze upon. They surround the Divine throne shouting their praises – 'Holy, holy is the Lord of Hosts. The whole Earth displays His glory.'

Every Seraph is possessed of three pairs of wings – one pair to conceal their face, a pair to hide their feet, and the other pair they use to fly.

Below the Seraphim are the Cherubim, who guard the way to the throne of God and the Tree of Life in the Garden of Eden. You would never mistake a Cherub for anyone else. For they have four heads – of a man, an ox, a lion, and an eagle – and four wings. And each wing is covered in eyes so they can see in every direction. They have the body of a lion but the legs of an ox. This much is well known from the Book of Ezekiel.

Below these are the Lordships, the angels that rule all the lower angels. They take the form of humans but possess a wonderful beauty. Lights shine from their heads. On their backs are large feathered wings.

The angels called the Powers order the movements of the heavenly bodies so the world moves as it should. Because they are warrior angels who fight evil spirits, the Powers wear helmet and armour, and carry a shield for defence and a weapon to smite the demons and the Evil Ones. It is said that Satan was supreme amongst the Powers until he fell.

In the third sphere are the Rulers and Archangels. Every nation and every force has the guardianship of a Ruler angel. They carry the conscience of the world and are the guardians of history. They share the power out between the nations and races.

But it is the plain, common angels who appear to mankind and help us in our daily lives. Every one of us has a personal angel who watches over us. But you must believe in that angel to gain his help. They may appear as ordinary people like you and me. Except they are often tall. They speak clearly but quietly. And their sweat smells sweet and polleny as honey. Still, it may happen that you meet your own angel, yet never know.

For two days I had kept my own company, trudging through woodland, observing the Liturgy of the Hours, and at dusk building myself a cover of branches strewn with ferns.

I did not make a fire for fear of showing myself and drawing company.

I welcomed the solitude. The encounter with Simon Mostly and my sore head had cautioned me. I needed to clear my mind, tidy my thoughts, and prepare myself to meet my fellow man, to defend myself from sinners.

On the third day, with the sun straight overhead, I wander into a glare of sunlight. I have come upon a pond in a clearing, and there see a figure kneeling, head to the water, pursed lips to the surface, lapping like a cat taking milk from a platter. They stand abruptly at the sound of my steps, as I break twigs underfoot, crunching the dry fallen leaves.

It is a slim, shortish being in a long dark woollen cloak, wrapped tight to the body, the head hooded. As I take a step closer, the figure takes a step backwards. I stop still. The figure pauses. We stand and watch each other, perhaps ten strides apart. I see the cloak, drawn tight to the chest, quiver to their quick breaths. I sense their squirrel twitchiness. I hear the rasp of their breath, sounding their fear. Of me.

When they speak it is with a shrill, trembly, breathy voice.

'I have a knife,' they say, 'and I will use it.'

'You will?'

'To dig your heart out of your chest, and roast it on a stick for dinner.'

'Peace be with you, friend,' I say, 'and God's blessings too.'

'And cut off your bollocks too. Then boil them with lovage and wild garlic.'

'And may Our Lord Jesus Christ watch over you.'

So, having made good our wary introductions, we continue to stare at each other in cautious curiosity.

The pink, fresh face of this wild cannibal is framed in coils of straw-coloured hair. Their hazel eyes glint in the sunlight. They dance fast as they look me over. They flicker over my face then take a downward tour of my frame.

'I'm not afraid of you,' the figure says. 'You're just a boy.'

'And I know who you are,' I reply promptly. For now I have the stranger's measure.

'You do?'

'Oh, yes,' I say.

For I have dreamed of people of this kind. And heard of them in travellers' tales. And witnessed them hand-illustrated in the manuscripts of Saint Odo.

'Who am I, then?'

'You must be a *woman*,' I say, unmasking her, 'of the female persuasion. Or something very similar.'

'Yes . . .' She blinks, then regards me sharply through narrowed eyes. 'It's true, I am.'

'I guessed so,' I say, 'soon as I saw you. For I am a keen observer of Nature in all Her manifestations, and I can read the signs anatomical.'

'Is that so?'

'Indeed. And I am happy to meet you. It has been my life's ambition to keep the company of a woman. And converse with her. And learn of all her customs. And hear her speak her mind. And find out all that makes her different from an inky scribe or common monk of the male tendency, and in whatever respects.'

Here, I keep silent on my false starts – with the intangible Succubus of my dreams.

108

This solid woman of my wakefulness puts her head to one side, and squints at me. She nibbles her lip. She eyes me hard and long. But as if she is looking downward, with curiosity, from a higher perch, the way you might regard a stubborn, wayward piglet, or a wilful chicken.

'Are you a simpleton?' she enquires.

'*Au contraire*,' I say. '*Je suis un savant.*'

She screws her face in puzzlement. 'Never mind. You may be simple as a donkey for all I care. But your looks are comely enough.'

'Comely?'

'You have a fine face, and a kind look to you. I trust your eyes of blue. If you were not a braying ass, I would call you handsome.'

'Handsome? Me?'

Now she has the advantage over me. She's taken me by surprise. No one has ever mentioned before that, judged in a kind light, I present a pleasant appearance.

But if a man is willing to listen, he can learn something new every day, even about the things he thinks he knows best, including his very own features.

I resolve to test the truth of her observations, when opportunity next arises, and take a good look at myself, and examine my reflection in the water for any signs of comeliness and nobility such as I have failed to notice before.

She seems to trust me better after a while. For though she keeps a few paces of distance between us, she consents to sit and talk.

109

She says her name is Cecilia, from the village of Ware. She had taken eggs to market in Chanse but found the town streets strangely empty. Then she learned that people were in hiding from each other, for the plague had come amongst them. So she had rushed away, to return home. But when she reached the outskirts of her village, folk came out to meet her, at a safe distance, and shouted at her to stay away, for fear she was tainted and brought the pox back from market with her. And they threw lumps of wood and stones her way, and shouted that she was a harlot and unclean, except her father who kept silent and turned away. And the loudest warned that if she came any nearer she would regret it, and feel their anger in earnest.

So now she is an outcast, alone in the woods. But she thought she would return soon to her village and, showing she is clean of the pox, be welcomed back, except she has heard that now the church bell is ringing often, and she has seen from a distance that there is much digging in the grave-yard. And wails carry on the breeze. So now she is afraid to return.

I tell her my tale too. But I tell it briefly. And prune many of the barbed briars of the story, so as not to strangle it with emotion, nor distract from the narrative, nor laden truth with useless baggage. I say that I worked as a scribe at a monastery but fled the plague, so now am homeless, and friendless too. I say a pair will be safer than one, and, God willing, we can find the ways to be strong together and help each other.

*

I felt myself oddly drawn to Woman. For some left-handed reason, which I could not name, but which drew me achingly, with the semblance of an itch I could not reach to scratch.

So I had resolved to pass some time with her, and she, for her reasons, never had me leave. Perhaps we both felt a kind and gentle, unspoken friendship, such as can form between brothers of the cloth, just passing silently through the cloisters, without thought of gain or advantage.

I spoke frankly to show her my good-will. I let her know I did not condemn her for her sex. For it was never her fault to be female, or any cause for blame, being merely the unfortunate, unchosen accident of her birth.

I remarked that, although Eve was made of Adam's rib, and tempted him to eat the forbidden fruit, so committing the original sin, and causing mankind to be thrown from the Garden of Eden, still this was never the dismal character of all women.

I observed that Mary, Mother of Christ, could be seen as the second Eve who redeemed woman, and made ample reparations for the sins of the first.

I mentioned that there were several holy and wise women well regarded by history, including Eleanor of Aquitaine, Hilda of Whitby and Hildegard of Bingen.

'Is that so?' said Cecilia. 'And, alongside your many rare wisdoms on dead women, do you have the common sense to gather wood and make a fire?'

I said yes, and continued that I had heard stories of

women who were as skilled as men at all manner of tasks – tending crops, minding animals, weaving cloth, brewing and baking – that drew upon craft, practice and custom rather than just cleverness, invention or strength.

'Yes?' Cecilia said, absent-minded. 'Can you go catch some food too?'

I said I could. For Fulco had taught me to tickle trout and snare small game.

I made several nooses out of twine that would tighten on an unwary foot, and set myself to wait.

But it was a while before I heard the shrieks of the hare, caught by a front foot, and found it leaping forward then jerking back, then leaping again, frothing at the mouth.

So I dispatched it with the blow of stone to the head. Then I blessed it, and thanked it for its gift of supper, and praised the Lord for His Creation.

Then I skinned and gutted it. I took the pieces proudly back to the girl – I handed them over, wrapped in large fern fronds – the ruby kidneys, the dark liver, the pink-speckled brains, the frothy lungs and the endless stringy bowels, together with the pearly bollocks and the eye-balls which returned to me a cold, harsh, shocked glare.

She looked to my offering then back to me.

'What?' she said. Her face displayed surprise, then annoyance, before moving quickly on to distaste.

'Hare,' I said, 'all the softest offals, fresh for cooking.'

'And the meat?'

'I left it where I caught it.'

'Why?'

'It was only the flesh and bones.'

'Yes,' she remarked, 'that's the bit I prefer.'

'Yes? In the monastery we only eat the offal. We cannot eat the meat. We must sell it to the rich or give it to the poor.'

'Says who?' she snaps.

'The Abbot,' I say.

Then I remember. All is changed. Now the Abbot is me.

'We are not sheep, grazing in a monastery garden,' she said. 'If you want to please me, you'd best go fetch the meat.'

And when I had retrieved it, she put the carcass on a stick and hung it between two wood props, over the flames of the fire.

It dripped its juices onto the embers, sparking and smoking, giving off a hazy incense more beguiling than rosemary, richer than cardamom, more teasing than musk, exotic as cloves.

'Mmm . . .' I savour the air. 'Just suppose it could taste as good as it smells.'

'Try it, then . . .' she said, handing me a scorched back leg.

It might be that I had eaten roast meat in my childhood, before I joined the monks. But I don't remember it.

And that day that woman, in the woods, gave me as much pleasure as I had ever embraced in my life before.

They say that tripe sausage is good, that blood pudding is very savoury, and molten cheese is unctuous, but I swear nothing better had ever passed my lips than that moist, fat-dripping, gravy-bleeding, flame-licked, smoked, roast hare.

All praise to the cony. Thanks to the woman. All glory to the Lord.

But it was not just her cooking that pleased me. With her hood down, and her head revealed, quite naked from the neck up, I had begun to notice aspects to her person that, though strange-looking, were strong and stirring.

When she was not looking my way, I watched her closely, to graze my eyes upon her form. I found myself regarding the small details of her face – the curlicue of an ear, the swell of a lip, the fine line of lashes, a coil of hair, the sheen of a cheek. And these brought pleasure to my eyes, and drew a smile to my face. I saw her features anew, as phenomena of natural interest, and possessed of odd beauty.

I was entranced.

Just as a doe, or wolf, or swan shows grace and beauty, in its cover, shapes and proportions, so did she. Then I came to note the music of her voice, for just as the night-ingale, mistle thrush or blackcap sound fine melodies, so did she. Then I came to savour the scents of her when she was close, for just as cloves, and coriander, and garlic fill the nose, and entertain the palate, so did she.

That first night we lay apart either side of our crackling fire.

The second night, we both grew cold and made a pact to lie close, and share our cover, with me behind, pressing into her back, snuggled tight to the warmth of her contours.

On the third night, the cold was crueller still and reached through to sting our bones.

We turned to face each other, arms about each other, hugging chest to chest.

Still, the cold grew sterner, setting its icy heart against us, as if to freeze our blood.

We were forced to put our faces close together, so our warm breaths were shared, then our hot mouths joined, and each felt the fiery pulse of the other, until we became one body, joined tight, melted into each other, like a beast with two backs, and just one set of fleas.

Then the cold was gone.

XII. The Seven True Differences between Man and Woman

So, by the happenchance of a meeting in the woods and a mercilessly chilly night, I began to fill a yawning void in my knowledge. For, despite passing my sixteenth year, and reading all the profound works of Saint Odo, and hearing all the wise teachings of Brother Fulco, I had gained only small, abstract knowledge of Woman. The little I had learned was just ill-founded rumours from celibate scholars, who had touched upon no skin but vellum, and dipped no more than their pen, wetting no more than their nib.

But now I had met Woman for myself and embraced her, in the raw flesh. And found her solid and tangible. Also sonorous. Warm to the touch. A fond taste upon my tongue, and aromatic. Sweet and salty, dry and wet, firm and soft. So I held her more and closer, avid in my curiosity.

And while it is true that she was just a single instance of Woman, and not the broad plurality of her gender, still I was able to grasp her every fine detail and make abundant rich discoveries across the continents of her surface, and committed every last patch of it to memory, even the remotest, shadiest, overgrown places, concealing the smallest cracks and crannies. So I should know the best routes and finest sites whenever I should have the fortune to visit again.

I found fine, rich delights in erasing my ignorance, in discerning the several ways the male and the female were alike in form, and the seven true ways they diverged, and the details of every difference, however slight, wherever I chanced upon them.

I discerned the Divine Design to fabricate the distaff – out of that spare rib of Adam's – in many ways alike to the male, yet fairer, smoother and softer and mossy-haired, with wider hips, plumper, cushioned curves, and gentle hillocks, with fewer hard, bony corners, differently perfumed, and without Man's braggart, dangling parts, as a hostage to fortune, and target to harsh buffets, in a hard, spiky world.

I took to my investigations with an aching vigour and an itching curiosity. There were times in my dark enquiry when my view was shaded or obscured – for the cold compelled us to keep ourselves most parts covered. Still, I believe that there was no portion or region of her fundament that passed untouched by my hand, no scent undetected by the nose, and no tang or flavour untasted by the tongue.

True, there were times when I lost the thread of my enquiry. For I went light-headed, in that state between dreams and wakefulness. I was distracted by a vague, jerky reverie. I was provoked by odd, illogical thrusts of desire. I was drawn by drunk attractions. Stupidly, I kept repeating my jerky awkwardness, over and over, again and again, before starting anew. I was straining to make up for all those lost, womanless years.

All that I belatedly discovered was good. I saw Man could not help but delight in the Divine Design, and rejoice in that fine fit to be found by joining Man and Woman.

Praise be to God.

In the morning, Woman surprised me anew.

I opened my eyes to the misty, dawning light to find her tousle-haired head close above mine, with her moist, sleep-crusted eyes smiling down at me, as her warm breath gusted my cheeks.

'Good morning, Husband,' she said.

'Good morning,' I said.

'You should call me Wife,' she said. 'Now we are married.'

'Married?' I said.

'In the sight of God,' she said. 'To be bonny and buxom at bed and at board, to love and to cherish, till death us part, according to God's holy ordinance; and thereunto I plighted thee my troth . . .'

I stayed silent and cast my mind back to the hours passed, to try to recall any declaration, or ceremony, or celebration of marriage. But none came to mind.

'What will my family say?' She threw her head back, giggling. 'When I return home with you, and say, "Look, here is my husband . . . who goes by the name of Jack . . . and is not the fool he first appears . . . who I found, wandering, woeful as a lost dog, with his tail between his legs, by Coppetts Pond, in the woods."'

'*Fool?*' I said. '*Woeful?*'

119

'So, you should give me a ring,' she said, 'to show the world we are married.'

'Yes?' I said.

'Like this one you wear on a cord around your neck.' She reached out to rub it between finger and thumb, then had it ride the tip of her finger. It was the bronze ring that Luke, my mother's father, gave to me, before he left me on the steps of the monastery.

'Yes?' I said.

'Look,' she said, twisting it onto her finger, having wet it with a gob of spit, 'how well it fits.'

'Yes,' I said. 'So it does.'

She spoke of where we might live. Close by her family. And how I might help her father tend the land and husband the beasts. She spoke of the sturdy, fine-looking children we might have, and the names we might give them. Like Ada, Adelina, Albreda, Alice, or Alban, Aldo, Ambrose, Anselm or August.

But I cautioned that perhaps we would not need so many child names and certainly not so very soon.

Saint Odo wrote of the future time when people trapped the *scintilla vitalis*, the vital spark, and carried it from place to place, in long tubes like umbilicals. This way, once connected, the inert and the dead came alive. Lights dazzled, fires burst ablaze, bells rang, voices sounded out of silence, pictures glowed out of darkness, water froze or turned into steam. Then everything was noise, light and movement. And darkness and silence were gone from the face of the world.

Later came the Age of the Metal Carts. These were covered, horseless carriages that ran on wheels, and farted black fumes, so even far in their wake you could smell they had travelled the road before, and fouled it for all that followed. They roared and growled. Sometimes they charged each other, head on, like rutting stags. Other times, they passed without any regard to each other, or else crowded together, in stationary flocks, like sheep.

The time of the Shape-Shifters was later still. These were folk who changed their human shape. For they were not satisfied with the visages and bodies God gave them, but paid craftsmen to change them. Even though it was heresy. Usurping the Almighty, never heeding that the human form was good and immutable, for it was fashioned to the Divine Design.

The Shape-Shifters paid skin-scribes to pierce them with needles dipped in ink, so they could be drawn upon, as if they themselves were some sheet of vellum. So they bore the dates of their children's birth, the names of their kin, the face of their loved one, secret signs, marks of the Devil, warnings for strangers to go away, flowers, eagles, sign-posts to their privates, or morals misspelled in foreign tongues, or invitations to intimacy, and pleasantries the first time funny.

And some paid blacksmiths to pierce them with studs, rings, bolts, through their faces, tongues, lips, cheeks, nipples and privities. So you could always find them in the dark, for they glinted back the moon-glow and rattled when they walked.

Others paid for doctors to stretch their cheeks taut as drum-skins. So they resembled skulls. And paid apothecaries to paralyse their face with poison, so they could not be ruffled by emotion. So feelings could not trespass across their visage, crease the surface and line them with experience. For they believed that growing old was a venial sin.

And they had their complexion painted orange. And raised their eyebrows, like flying buttresses, vaulting towards the heavens. And swelled their lips like the pout of a trout. And swelled their bosoms larger than wet-nurses'. And had the flesh sucked out of their bellies and pushed back into their buttocks instead, so then their lumps were back to front. And snipped their privates and bleached their bottoms.

So some parts of their corpus were made larger. And some made smaller. And some flatter. And some bumpier. And some lighter and some darker. And some harder and some softer. And some longer and some shorter.

It was like the Sumptuary Law we have now. Just as only the rich or powerful may wear fur, fine fabric or purple, so only the wealthy could join the Tribe of the Skull. So fine looks became a purchase. And the poor folk were excluded from the parade of beauty, left looking as plain and alive as God had shaped them. For they could not afford the medicine to make them look like rich, embalmed corpses.

But, oh, woe.

The worst came upon us.

122

We had been followed. Cecilia and I.

A terrible evil had crept up on us.

On the third day my new wife woke vexed and listless, her forehead beaded with sweat, her teeth chattering, with a violent heat to her body. She had a terrible throbbing ache to her head, she said, and was too weak to rise.

There was a rich, putrid tang that I had not scented on her before. But I had smelled it on my departed brothers when I laid them to rest.

May God have mercy on their souls.

'Oh, wife . . .' I sighed. 'Dear wife . . . you can't go so very soon.'

We had only been married a couple of days. And now she was all but lost to me.

'Husband?' she asked, croaky and weak.

There were lumps on her neck the size of pigeon eggs, and more nested in her arm-pits and groin.

She bent sideways to a bout of coughing, and a treacly black stuff trickled from the side of her mouth.

I saw a couple of fleas jump forth from the valley between her breasts, leaping an arc to the ground, and I thought of them as desperate mariners, throwing themselves to the broad ocean, fleeing the sinking ship.

All day, as I tended her, the buboes slowly swelled and grew darker. The tips of her fingers and her nose became purpled. There was the smell of the black rot, eating its way through her, from the insides to the surface.

'I feel sick unto death,' she whispered, blowing bloody bubbles. Every word a struggle for breath.

'Will you confess?' I asked. 'Take care for your immortal soul.'

So, she mumbled the worst she had ever done. Which was little enough, but laboured in its coming, on brief, brave gusts of shame.

Except that she confessed she had thrown the two skulls I bore in my bag into the pond. She said they scared her, and made her uneasy. She feared they'd bring bad luck. For it was sinister, she said, to travel with dead men's bones. And did I mind?

So I prayed for Saint Odo to forgive her. Twice. For she knew not what she did.

Then I spoke the Absolution and drew the sign of the cross on her forehead.

May the Almighty and Merciful God grant you pardon,
    and remission of your sins.
May the Almighty God have mercy on you, and bring
    you to life everlasting. Amen.

Shortly after, I heard her final snort, which was her soul departing, in a rush. So I watched her go, riding the breeze, to eternity, blown out in a fine, blood-speckled spray of snot from her nose.

Then I closed the lids of her eyes.

Then I cried.

And, after that, I howled.

A distant fox answered me. A brother in yearning. A dog-fox calling out for his vixen.

*

I dug my wife under. But I saw it was not her any more – only the rattle-bag of an empty husk. Her spirit was gone elsewhere. I placed a wooden cross on the grave and gouged out the name Cecilia on the cross-piece, and below it in smaller script I scratched, 'Brief, beloved wife of Jack'.

I fell asleep, to the tang of my hot salty tears.

But next morning I woke refreshed by hope, with a calm contentment. A clarity had come to my muddled mind. My thoughts flowed limpid and fresh, the sediments settled.

I realised that everything has a purpose, shaped by His Divine will. And nothing is for nothing.

The pox was dogging me, claiming everyone I met. Yet always leaving me to live. Which I took as a sign that the pestilence and I were entwined, fellow travellers, with our fates joined. I faced up to the facts of my life. I saw the pattern that they revealed. How I had been fathered not by a peasant but by a Papal messenger, and was delivered up to a monastery, gifted to learn the wisdoms of Saint Odo, taught the science of Brother Fulco, trained to treat the sick. So I realised then that I was special and chosen. That I was here for His purpose, and had been given a task, in order to follow the pestilence, find its cause, and thereby its cure. That man should learn his moral lesson and regain the love of the Lord.

Praise be to God.

Any word is two words. And any meaning is the difference between them. Brother Fulco had taught me so. For after Grammar, Rhetoric, Gardening and Gymnastics, he went on to teach me Semantics, the study of meanings.

So he showed me that once you give birth to a single word – like *alive*, you have brought to life its opposite – *dead*.

And once you have the opposite, by implication you create its contrary, what it is not – *un-dead*, like demons and spirits, and then the opposite of that contrary – *un-alive*, like the ghosts.

So then, out of one word, you have made four words – the quartet of possibility – *the alive, the dead, the un-dead, the un-alive*.

Which allows for six further meanings. The combinations. For some things are jumbled, like those that are both living and dead. And the un-alive and the un-dead, and the dead and the un-alive. And so on.

This way you can comprehend Our Lord Christ who was dead but rose again alive, departed souls that are gone from life but alive in Purgatory, Heaven or Hell, and the lost, shocked souls, like ghosts and ghouls, who died but cannot free themselves from the realm of the living to find their proper homes beyond.

The mind reaches out for strange consolations. I conjectured that though my dear wife Cecilia was dead, still she was alive . . . and also alive and dead when I looked at it sideways . . . and moreover both un-dead and un-alive in another way of seeing things . . . and yet alive and

126

un-dead, locked in my memory, and tied to my heart by love, attached to my desire by strands of longing . . . furthermore alive yet un-alive to Purgatory, having died well – confessed and absolved.

So now she was more than alive, and shimmered into several meanings, like the lights of the rainbow scattered by a prism.

All of which made me feel better, and my wife closer. And distant too. And yet both together.

For Brother Fulco had taught me another thing.

He showed me that any word is three words. For any word creates its opposite. And between them there must lie the middle-term that joins and resolves them.

So between sky and sea comes the earth. Between day and night comes dusk. Between night and day comes dawn. Between love and hate is indifference. Between God and man comes Jesus Christ, both human and Divine. And between Heaven and Earth are the angels as messengers to us.

Between woman and fish comes the mermaid. Between woman and bird is the harpy. And between man and goat is the faun. And between man and horse is the centaur.

So the scholars say. That Our Lord left no opposition unresolved. Every two dissimilar things will find their mix on God's Earth. Only sometimes you must look hard to find them. And sometimes it is better not to lift the stone. Or wander into that dark place.

XIII. I Dance Barnaby and
Sup at the Mossy Well

Now I walked out with purpose. And without fear.

I saw that I was some way joined to this pestilence, by some invisible tie, and that it had the power to find me, wherever I went. It would not hurt me now. For I had fought it the first time and survived. The second time it visited, it left me barely touched. Only the sweats and headaches bothered me. The blue spots were small and largely gone.

So, whatever the pestilence sought, it wasn't me.

I was no longer afraid of contagion in crowded places. I took to the wider paths. I let the Lord guide my feet.

Next day, I find He leads me to the inn of the Seven Stars in the village of Ravenstone. It seems as good a place as any. He always has His reasons.

The inn is crowded. And I had forgot how strong a herd of folk can smell in their plurality – of warm, damp armpits, excrement, rotten teeth, mildewed clothes, woodsmoke, simmering pottage, and stale spilled ale. There is a smoky fug and a clamour of shouting, laughter, singing, fiddle and drum.

I sit myself on a bench alongside an old man, hunched smiling over his pot of ale. He says his name is Michael and that he is a travelling cobbler.

'They say there's a pox abroad,' I say, 'but folk seem happy. Has the news not reached here yet?'

'The plague?' He shrugs. 'What can we do?'

'Repent,' I suggest. 'Suffer. Pray for God's forgiveness . . . Hide . . . Flee.'

'I'll tell you how it is . . .' He pauses to raise his eyes heavenward. 'There has never been a more dire and terrible happening, not in Northampton, not in the surrounding parts, nor in cobbling in particular.'

'Cobbling?'

'I am a shoe-maker.'

'Yes?'

'And do you know who buys shoes since the plague struck?'

'Who?'

'Nobody.' He smacked the table-top with the flat of his hand.

'Why?'

'Those departed this life don't need shoes. The rest are too busy fleeing. Besides, the dead only make matters worse.'

'They do?'

'Yes, for they leave their footwear behind them. So, now, there are many more shoes than feet . . .'

I nod my understanding.

'And if someone brings me their shoes to repair . . .'

'Yes?'

'They rarely come back to pay for my labour.'

'No?'

'For, likely as not, they are dead by the morrow . . .'

'Oh,' I observe.

'People are dying too fast to bury them. The bodies are stacked in piles outside the boundary walls. The foul stench of decay carries everywhere. Crows, dogs and wild pigs feed on the corpses and scatter the pieces. So, on your doorstep, you might find here a human head, and here a leg, half-eaten . . . Maybe some thief has stolen the shoe.'

I shake my head at his sorry account.

'Do you know who supplies me with shoe-leather now?'

'Who?'

'Nobody . . . For the tanners are all dead or fled . . . And when you go to church to pray for salvation, there's no priest. For the clergy have died too, catching the pox, attending the dying. And the doctors have all run away. For they knew they could do nothing, except save themselves. And the beasts are gone wild, uncared for in the fields, while the crops have rotted, for no one has harvested them. And whole villages are abandoned. While thieves and cut-throats rule the roads. And often the good die ahead of the wicked. So justice is dying too.'

'Yes?' I say.

'For the pestilence has no mind who it takes. Be they good or bad, young or old. All end up in the charnel shop.'

'It's a sorry state of affairs,' I agree.

'So, I don't save myself by being good. I don't risk myself by being bad. Plague takes you or leaves you. Until it decides, you might as well take what pleasures you find.'

Then he upturns his tankard to show me it is empty,

131

and winks vigorously to convey he is willing to sup still more.

'Maybe,' I say, 'I could offer you a fill of ale?'

I suppose my brief marriage had changed me. For I was less the boy and more a man – no longer a reclusive monk, but now a freeman of the world. I was a bud opening to the summer sun, poised to spread my petals and bloom. Although I had been only briefly married, I was still tied by an invisible bond, a fierce devotion to my dear, departed wife, so alive in my heart as she stood there, apart in eternity, in the interminable, sorry queue of Purgatory.

Ah. How I missed her – her sweet, demanding companionship and the beauty of her form, so artfully devised Divine to please the senses. Seeing the women at the inn, in their bonnets, hurrying hither and thither, upstairs, downstairs, now hand in hand with a man, now without one, now so soon with another, I naturally thought to my loss.

I asked my companion who these women were.

He said, 'Those in bright dresses are Hurdy Gurdy girls who dance with the lonely, for a fee. And those with the striped bonnets are ladies of the bed-chamber, who will take you to their naked bosom if you are lonelier still.'

Then it struck me there might be some hapless compensation to be snatched, briefly, with one of these women, if only as a sacrament, in honour and remembrance of my poor, departed wife, Cecilia, and the times I spent between her spread thighs, pressed to her warm, silken, pliant belly.

One noted my gaze, read my curiosity, returned a smile, nodded and approached me.

'I am Constance,' she said. 'You can lie with me if you like.'

I asked if that would make us married, for I did not want to commit again too soon, or contract to purchase uncertain goods. Not for life. For I had found myself caught in that man-trap once before.

'Not if you pay me,' she said, 'for then I will be your Molly and you will be my John.'

We agreed a contract, there and then, to go upstairs and lie together, to tie ourselves in a carnal tangle, so that I might enjoy her every surface, and she might benefit a whole half-penny, non-returnable and paid in advance, which she quickly stowed, God knows where. For it was promptly lost in a pink and white blur of flesh and cloth.

I was able to broaden and further my acquaintance with Woman, although the enterprise was not long begun before it was done. For we went about things briskly and directly, without preamble, or any delay for anticipation or conversation. And she was up and away at the first, quick sneeze of my loins, and sprung off the bed, as quick as a terrier sighting a rat. As if all our business was done.

I spoke to her naked rear as she dressed, and admired the fleshy fruit of her form. With her head bowed forward, her top half took the fruity shape of a pear. The tied-tail of her hair formed a stalk. Her back was milk-white, freckled with amber splodges. I saw the dark tufts of her calyx, the palace of pollination, between her splayed legs. I had learned something new. I realised that, of course, just like monks in the bath-house, all woman were strangely, determinedly different in the ways they were alike.

You may come confident, laden with expectation of what you will find, but you are sure to meet some mood, opinion, desire, proportion, texture, touch, taste, blemish, beauty or scent for which you were never prepared, having never met before.

I told Constance she seemed some ways different to the one other woman I had lain with, yet several ways similar too.

She was more solidly constructed than my willowy wife, Cecilia, may she rest in peace, and had stouter, tree-trunk legs and heavier, pendulous breasts. Besides, she sprouted thicker fur, more widely, densely spread.

'Yes?' she enquired, wriggling into her smock. But she did not seem eager to hear the full yield of my anatomical observations.

She simply remarked that, for my part, I was much like other men, if scrawnier, smaller, pocked, and quicker about my mattress work than many.

Then she slapped her left buttock sharply and swivelled round to eye the reddened spot.

'I hope you have not given me fleas,' she said.

'Would you say you are like most other women?' I asked. 'In the way you are designed and made flesh by the Architect Divine.'

'I believe so,' she said. 'None say otherwise. And many men have been and gone. They climb aboard. They bounce around. They grunt and groan. They come, then go. Let them squirm and squirt and they won't complain.'

I explained that, for me, the body of a woman was still a new-found land. I thanked her for her revelations, time and industry. I said I had much enjoyed her. Every last region of her candid terrain.

Before, behind, between, above, below.

But curiosity still clutched me. I guessed there were things undone.

So I asked if she knew any other sins a man could contract with a woman, besides the single one she had just shown me. And so very quickly.

She squinted at me and cupped her chin in her palm.

'Have you not tried gobbledegoo?' she asked.

I shook my head.

'Or the deed of deepest darkness?'

'No. I believe not.'

'Flipsum-flopsum, or rump-scuttle?'

'Not those, neither,' I conceded.

'Stiff quiff?'

'No.'

'Bardash or lick-spigot?'

'I think not,' I confessed. 'These are new-sounding pastimes that mean nothing to me.'

They struck no chords, rang no bells, and they had passed entirely unremarked in the conversations of my brothers in Christ, or in the writings of Saint Odo.

'So you have never danced Barnaby, greased the goose or supped at the mossy well?'

135

'No,' I conceded. 'For, if I had, I would surely remember.'

She looked at me with a sorry sympathy. She rolled her eyes upwards. She clucked. She shook her sad head.

'I cannot teach you *every last thing*,' she said, 'but I suppose we could make a start at least . . .'

'You'd find me grateful . . .'

'But nothing is for nothing . . .' she warned.

'Another half-penny?'

'Three whole pennies,' she said decisively, 'and I will trouble your innocence all the way till dusk.'

So, I paid. And she was better than her word.

And, by the time dark fell, I was weary, contented, even beyond my desires, and a wiser man too. For there is a craft to everything and possibilities you never dreamed of, if only you take the time to find them, or open yourself up to learn.

XIV. The Sin-Eater

In satisfying one hunger, I had released another. And a thirst. So I took those appetites downstairs and bought a bowl of barley pottage, a platter of buttered cabbage tops, and a jug of ale.

The table quivers and creaks as a man sits himself down on the other side. I sense a gaze fall upon me.

I raise my eyes to meet his. One of his eyes is the palest blue, the other the deepest brown. He has a bushy head of ginger hair.

A shiver rides my spine. The back of my neck prickles. There's a loud crackle in my ears.

He is the man of the woods, who calls himself Simon Mostly. I feel a wild clamour of anger and fear.

I think of my aching head, empty sack, stolen belongings, and the burnt *Book of Life*.

But he greets my glare with a wide, open smile, leaning forward, shaking his head in delighted surprise.

'Praise be to God,' he says, 'you're alive still. I feared they'd killed you.'

'They?' I say. 'Who?'

'The villains who attacked us,' he says, 'who crept up behind us and fell upon us with clubs.'

'They attacked you too?'

'They used me horribly.' He wipes his cheek with his one good hand, smearing some sudden tears in dirty smudge. 'They took me to their camp. They hung me by my foot from a tree and beat me with staves.'

'Why?'

'They thought I had money hidden. They wanted to know where.'

'Why would they think you had money?'

'I am well known hereabouts, for my special trade.'

'What trade?'

He winks by closing his blue eye. Then he twitches his left cheek and feels where his missing ear should be. Then he winks by closing his brown eye.

'I lift sin from the wicked,' he says. 'I clean souls.'

'You do?'

'It is a lonely dismal trade. But it pays me solid pennies.'

'It does?'

'You remember confiding, in the woods, that you were a squalid sinner?'

I confess that I do. That I am. And that the count of my sins is rapidly rising.

He nods. 'It shows in your troubled eyes, and along the creases of your forehead, and in the tappety-tap of your worried fingers.'

'It does?'

'As clear as sporting sack-cloth and ashes. But have no care,' he says, 'for I have a cure. I can lift your sins from you. Then you will be rid of them, for all eternity.'

'How can you do that?'

'I will *eat* them for you,' he confides. 'For by trade I'm a Sin-Eater.' He makes a quick chewing sound, then gulps, with a sustained pretence of swallowing something awkward, reluctant to descend his gullet.

'Eat them?'

'All of them . . . Quick as you like . . . For a price . . .'

'How?'

'Spread them on a crust of bread . . . or a whole loaf, if it's needed. It depends how many sins you have to your name.'

'You misunderstand me, friend,' I say, 'for my sins are not solid, edible things. But are stubborn smudges and sticky stains to my soul that cannot be erased, except by the reparation of suffering, or by the forgiveness of Jesus who, if he wills it, can wash them clean away.'

'Jesus is all very well,' Simon Mostly concedes, 'in His own particular way. But I have a different cure. As soon as I have eaten your sins, and taken them out from you, into myself, you will feel their leaden weight lift from your spirits. You will feel free. You will feel clean. For you will no longer be accountable for those heavy, ugly, shameful sins draped over your conscience. For I will have taken them from you.'

'Have you eaten many sins?' I ask. 'In your time?'

'I have eaten sackfuls and barrow-loads . . .' He holds his hand flat to his gullet, to show me how full of sin he is. 'I have eaten sins large and small, of every sort. Men's sins and women's sins, baby sins and senile sins, lords' sins and peasant sins, venial sins and mortal sins, sins of the flesh,

139

sins of the mind, and sins of the heart. Wet sins, moist sins, and dry-as-dust sins. Light sins and heavy sins. Sins too paltry to mention and sins too vile to understand.'

'How do they taste?' I ask.

'All are different. Every sin has its special savour, its unique scent, and its own rare texture. But, you can rely on it, most are tough on the teeth. They take a deal of chewing. And then they take a lot of swallowing. So, I usually have to wash them down with ale . . . or mead to cancel the bitterness. I would say that murder and heresy are the worst sins – to chew over and to swallow at least . . .'

'What will happen to you?' I ask. 'Now you have taken so many different sins inside you?'

'Eternal damnation, I suppose . . . But at least I've helped my fellow man.' He shrugs. He narrows his watery, dull eyes. 'There's nothing I can do. For I have forgotten now which sins I ate, and when, and in what order. So even if I emptied my soul of all those I knew, the most part would still remain.'

'I will pray for you, then,' I offer.

'You will not . . .' Anger flushes his face. He presses his nose to mine and glowers gimlet-sharp, deep into my eyes.

'No?'

'No,' he growls, then bangs his fist on the table. 'For I am the only man allowed to sell cures for sin in this place. It is a bargain I made with the inn-keeper.'

I hurry to apologise. 'Of course, there would be no cost to you.'

140

'Yes?' He howls his indignation. 'Then how do I make my living? If you start doing my work for free?'

I kept my distance from him, but stayed on at the inn.

I felt sickly still. My body seemed ferociously hot. A small lump grew in my left arm-pit, then changed its mind and shrank away. So I was able to rest my weary body, add a little bulk to my starved form, and sleep safe, beneath a thatch, out of the winds and rains.

I got to eat more and different meats I had never tasted before. Like bacon, which may be the finest food in Christendom, bar none.

It comes fried in thin slices from the flesh of oak-smoked ribs of a pig, hung from a rafter to mature with age.

And there was mutton which is hewn from dead, stewed sheep, and beef which is carved from the carcasses of dead cows. And kid from goats. Potted duck from throttled ducks. And roasted chicken, whose name explains it all.

And when I was not wasting my pennies, trying new meats, basted in steaming gravies, or baked in hot pies, or served on bread platters, all delicious, I was able to make further conversation with Constance. And also speak with Patience. And then, by chance, with Alice too. At a price.

On the third day, I visit Constance in her chamber, and find her out of sorts and strangely lethargic. She is burning hot. She complains of fierce prickles, like arrows through her belly. She says she cannot rise from her bed. Her breath smells of sulphur. She tries to vomit but nothing

141

will come. She says a blacksmith's hammer is clanging away in her head.

Nestling in the hairs of her under-arm lies a small bluish lump like a pigeon's egg.

Yes, a bubo. For the plague has caught her.

It has crept up on us again, slithering silent, behind our backs, without warning.

At prayer in my monastery, it finds me.

Hiding deep in the woods, it finds me.

At rest in the tavern, it finds me.

It hounds me remorselessly, like a hunter, sniffing my scent, dogging my tracks. Never more than three days behind. And I can't think how to out-run it.

In the inn the cry goes up, 'The pox is here . . .'

And the inn empties. The drunks, fornicators, gamblers, ladies of the bed-chamber, swindlers, thieves, musicians all spill out and away, gone as quick as the ale gushes from a toppled tankard.

Gervase the inn-keeper and Luke the stable-boy carry Constance down from her bed, their hands wrapped in rags to prevent contamination. They cover her in sacking, so the sight of her cannot infect them, and lay her on straw in a corner of the stable. They quickly discuss whether the horses and goats are safe, or if the beasts can contract the pox too. Then they are gone, without a backward look.

I stand there alone with Constance groaning, splayed limp at my feet.

'Be strong,' I say, 'I will doctor you well. I will do my best to save you . . .'

I kneel to feel the furnace of her forehead and smell the rotten eggs of her breath.

I wonder what Brother Fulco would do, and think back to the basic rules of medicine. Then I know what to do.

i. If it is hot, it must be made cool.
ii. If it is dry, it must be made wet.
iii. The four humours must be re-balanced.
iv. The stomach and bowels must be emptied of their sick yield.
v. Much lettuce should be eaten, for it is cleansing and curative.
vi. The bloods must be let to the point of causing faintness.
vii. The incision should be made at the point of greatest pain.
viii. Any boils and buboes must be lanced to drain away their poison.

'Don't worry,' I say, 'I'm here to bring you comfort and cure. First we must take off your clothes to let your roasting body cool . . . and douse you with cold water to keep it temperate . . . Then we must make you vomit . . . and empty your bowels. Before we bleed you . . .'

Her eyes flutter fast. Her lips twitch, but no words come out.

I slide the purging pellet between her lips, past her

resisting teeth, and hold her mouth closed till she swallows. And, sure enough, she is soon twisted sideways, vomiting. But her sick is black and bloodied, which is a poor signification.

I take out my pocket knife, wipe it clean, then sharpen it on a stone.

'Tell me,' I ask, stroking her burning forehead to soothe her, 'I must make a cut. So tell me where it hurts the worst?'

XV. If Your Eye Offend You,
Pluck it Out

I had found a new vocation. I had been called to it by the Almighty. I was become a plague doctor.

To call himself full physician, a doctor must have attended some university – Oxford, Salerno, Montpellier, Paris, Bologna perhaps, or Padua – following his studies there for seven full years, and become ordained as a priest in the meantime.

So my place in God's scheme fell short of this. Still, I was trained as surgeon and apothecary. I could dose and bleed, cut with a knife, sew and saw upon patients, which the physicians disdained as the manual job of a labourer – the work of mere barbers and butchers.

Fulco had taught me hard and taught me long. I knew the liturgy of medicine. To begin, the doctor must ask any patient if they have committed some grievous recent sin, for which this malady is God's retribution and just punishment.

If the sufferer admits so, there may be no need for earthly medicines. Confession, suffering, prayer, abasement, penitence may suffice. Provided the Lord, in his kindness, relents. It's understood that leprosy is God's way of marking out those unrepentant in heresy or lust. The Lord depicts their sin, marking their hands and faces to show the ugliness of their souls. But often the sufferer may honestly answer, 'No.' He has not sinned his way into sickness. The illness may not be any Divine punishment for sin, but come of some turbulence in the natural order. A malign conjunction of the planets. A dismal mismatch of numbers. An imbalance in the humours.

The numerology of the patient's name may give indication of their likely fate. You must convert the letters to their corresponding numbers and calculate their totality. Then add those together. And so on. Until you reach just one single number between one and nine. And blessed is the sufferer whose final number is three, seven or nine.

A prayer may help, addressed to the patron saint of the organ in question, or any holy figure associated with the disease. So invite the help of Saint Lazarus for leprosy, Saint Agatha for breasts, Saint Jude for desperate remedies, Saint Anthony for skin disease, Saint John the Apostle for burns, Saint Anne for the barren.

Then check the celestial aspects, looking to the alignments of those stars relevant to the body parts and illness. For, with the moon in Scorpio, a surgeon would be foolish to operate upon the organs of generation. Likewise, in Leo, no treatment should be given to the chest.

After which, it is wise to consult the calendar to see if it is a dismal, perilous day, with the waxing or waning of the moon when that treatment is sure to fail.

I attended Constance closely for two full days but, despite my enduring presence, best surgeries, bleedings and purgings, and the best wisdoms of medicine, garnered over centuries, collected from three continents, I could not halt her suffering. Death had her.

Nor could I save any of the others who stayed on at the inn – the inn-keeper, Gervase, his wife, Gregory the smith, Davy the cooper, Patience, Alice. All who caught the pestilence suffered the same initial symptoms – shivers, fever, headaches, vomiting, loose bowels, terrible weakness, and reeking of a putrid stench. Then there were two ways the disease progressed. Some coughed up blood, sneezed it from their nose, and drowned from their own fluids in their lungs, and were dead within two days.

Others grew swellings in their neck, under-arms and groin. The buboes grew from acorn size to swell big as apples, and darkened from red to purpley-black. Then black patches might appear on their skin. Their nethers – fingers, toes, nose – would turn black with rot. This was the slower route to death and could take up to five days. Though some could fall ill and die in the very same day.

The first form I called the *plague pulmonaris*. The latter I termed the *plague bubonic*. Together they were the twins we called the Black Death. If the two forms were not the exact same malady, but attacking the body in two different routes, then they were brothers, carried the same taint and arrived together, with the same first signs. But one took itself to the lungs, and the other laid siege to the lacteal nodes.

Then I thought to the direction and speed it travelled.

The pox followed me close, but always behind. It took some slower path. So I kept ahead of it until I paused some place. Then it always caught me up in two or three days.

And the plague had a determined direction. It preferred to travel north. For it arrived first in Sicily, then passed up to Florence and Marseilles, then onwards and upwards, through France to Normandy, then to the Channel, then to the south coast, then upwards through England.

It was said that the cause of the miasma was celestial, from the strange, rare conjunction of Jupiter, Saturn and Mars. Warm and humid Jupiter had drawn up evil vapours from the earth. Mars – hot and dry – had ignited the vapours, releasing the plague. And, as we all know, Saturn adds evil wherever it goes.

I thought too of the signs left by the lesser beasts. Fleas and lice fled the human afflicted, in search of safer terrain. Dead mice and rats appeared in the wake of the pestilence, lumped and speckled black, as if they were poxed too.

Then I thought what further cures I could try.

If it was a miasma, it was carried by the wind from the south. From this came the clear logic to keep all southward-facing doors and windows closed, blocking ventilation save from the north.

If the miasma entered through the lungs, it would be safer for us to limit our exertions, so reducing the volume of airs we drew into our lungs.

I found myself alone at the inn. Those that had not fled were dead.

Travellers had moved on. The villagers were hidden in their dwellings, having bolted themselves in. They would not open their shutters or doors. When I passed nearby they howled threats, and shouted I should be gone.

When people saw me coming on the paths, they hurled stones to halt me, or rushed off to the side, to give me a wide berth. And they cast foul words. They called me unclean because I had been with the sick. They were not weighed down by reason. They had no knowledge of medicines. They feared I somehow carried the pox.

The village was lost. Those who did not leave would most likely die.

I could tell I was not wanted. For folk hurled threats my way when I showed myself in a window or doorway of the abandoned inn, saying they would burn the inn down around me if I did not leave. And nailed a dead cat to the door with its throat cut, and its entrails hanging out like links of sausage. And I knew it was an ill-intentioned gesture, addressed directly to me.

So I knew they never valued the medicine I brought to them, so it would be better for all if I moved on. So I left that night, by lifting the cellar hatch, in the deepest dark, wriggling on my belly till I had passed through the long grass into the swaying shadows of the wind-blown woods, to the welcoming hoots of an owl.

On the first day travelling west (for I sought to feint, to confuse the pox), I met a group of folk travelling the path towards me.

They meandered in a single, clumsy, halting column, a dozen of them, shabbily dressed in sacking and coarse, torn cloth, long unwashed. They were joined in a snaking line, each with his hands resting on the shoulders of the one in front, each with a bandage wrapping his eyes. A stout man in a crimson jerkin and leather cap took the lead, so he appeared as the gaudy head of a long, patchy, segmented insect.

The leader sang the verse –

> The town we left was full of dead
> Fat flies fed on the corpses' heads
> Doctors purged, dosed and bled
> And proved by sound deliberation
> It was the fault of some constellation
> Then dropped dead, past disputation.

Then the followers found voice to sing a chorus, but in poor, discordant unison, as they swayed along, moving their feet in time to their rhyme –

> Black Death, you can't have us.
> You can beckon and smile,
> but we'll never see you.

'Hail, Brother,' I say to the head of the snaking beast, as we pause on the path to greet each other.

'Whoa,' he calls, as if addressing a horse, so those behind him should halt and fall silent.

'Well met, stranger,' I say. 'I am Jack Fox, from the monastery at Whye.'

'I am Lucas the One-Eyed,' he says. 'And this . . .' He gestures down to the dusty path. 'The road is my home.'

'And your companions?' I ask. Although I have guessed already from their bandaged heads.

'These are a dozen none-eyed folk,' he waves behind him, 'who have no sight between them. So they are blind as a litter of new-born puppies.'

'That is a large gathering,' I remark, 'of the blind. How is it you only have one eye between you all?'

'They have rescinded their eyes to protect themselves from the plague.'

'Why?'

'Why?' He grimaces and shakes his head at my stupidity. 'Because they would rather live than see.'

'How so?' I ask.

Lucas shakes his head in disbelief at my ignorance. He says it is well known that the plague is spread by sight. The spirit of the pox leaps out from the eye of the sick man, into the eye of the healthy. Thus those who cannot see the illness cannot become ill themselves.

'And yet you, yourself, chose to keep one eye,' I observe. 'Does that not lay you open to the risk of contagion?'

'Some are born to lead. Some to follow. My people need me. They need the foresight and wisdom of my one good eye. I am their king. I see the way forward for all of them. But if I am in danger of seeing something I should not, I cover my good eye with this patch.' And so saying he draws a piece of leather, like the blinker for a horse, over the right side of his face.

151

'That's a handsome patch,' I agree. 'And suits you well.'

'If you wish it . . .' The one-eyed man gives me a kind, concerned smile. 'I can save you too.'

'Save me?'

'I can save you from your eyes, as I did for the others. It's quickly done. It is worth the pain to gain certain life . . .'

'How do you do that?' I have no wish for this surgery myself, but my doctor's curiosity insists to know.

'I would dig out your eyes with a knife. Then cauterise the wounds with a red-hot iron.'

And, as he says this, he sways forward, clutching my tunic at the neck, and draws his sheep's horn-handled knife close to my cheek, narrowing his eye, to assess where to strike, as he quotes me the scripture, his hot breath gusting onto my cheek.

'Matthew, chapter five, verse twenty-nine,' says he –

'*And if thy right eye offend thee, pluck it out, and cast it from thee: for it is profitable for thee that one of thy members should perish, and not that thy whole body should be cast into Hell.*'

So, fearing for my sight, I promptly raise my knee upwards, firmly between his legs, and he yelps at this assault upon his privities, and we fall down, then roll around, with me on him, then he on me, until I can reach out for a handful of earth to rub into his one good eye.

'Stop,' he calls to me, righteously aggrieved. 'You're blinding me.'

He lets me loose, to reach for his face. I am free. I am up and away.

152

'Stop him,' he calls to his chain of companions.

They are in a semi-circle around me. They can hear me close from my panting breath. They edge forwards towards me drunkenly, reaching out with their arms, stumbling on the uneven ground, but I am off and away, ducking under their groping arms, back the way I came, running hard.

'Stop, stop,' I hear the fallen man call, 'I can save you . . . Give them up. Give me your eyes . . . Or they'll be the death of you . . .'

And as I flee, I am struck by a pity for all those stumbling behind me, who have chosen to be blind. For I think they are wrong, that if they cannot see the plague, it cannot see them.

XVI. We Happy Band of Pilgrims

The next day I came upon the tail of a column of pilgrims, twelve altogether, gathered for safety and strength in numbers, making their way to the shrine of the Virgin at Walsingham.

I enquired if I might join their number. And after gathering some moments in a muttering huddle, they allowed that I could. I guess my mildness, youth and healthy appearance led them to trust me, and suppose I might be more use to them than burden.

We trudged, heads down, most often in silence, hugging our sadness, for some had lost their loved ones, many had fled their homes, and all feared the sudden, fatal touch of the plague.

Matthew the mason declared that the world was ending and this was the Final Reckoning, when all our souls would be weighed in His balance. It was said every soul would be tested against the holy feather, whose weight it should not exceed. Or else there was Hell to pay.

On the first night, after our supper – a harvest of hedgerow plants, a badger, freshly deceased, which we roasted in clay, and oat porridge – we all sat talking around our fire. Jude, the dealer in relics, sought me out and showed me his wares.

He laid a square of pristine white cloth on the ground, then opened a series of small brown leather pouches, withdrawing each object with great delicacy, beside a show of reverence, making the sign of the cross and gazing heavenwards with his eyes closed.

He said that I must forgive him the poverty of his wares, for he had left his most precious items at home, for safe-keeping – these being a piece of the clay left over after God had made Man, and the skin of the snake from the Garden of Eden.

Nonetheless, he said, he still had relics of great rarity and power.

He promised that the purchase of any such would protect me against the plague, defend me against evil-doers, and spare me ill-fortune.

The first object was a narrow glass vial, holding a dark brown dust, sealed with a cap of beeswax.

'What's that?' I asked.

'Can you guess?' he asked. 'You'll be surprised, for it is very precious.'

'Tell me,' I said. 'What is it, then?'

'It is milk from the breast of the Virgin Mary. Over the centuries, it has dried to this holy powder.'

'Indeed?' I said. Then we both pondered it awhile in silence.

'And this . . .' He pointed to something that looked like the end-piece of a sage-speckled pork sausage.

'Yes?'

'Is the foreskin of Saint Peter, the fisherman.'

'Truly?' I said. 'You surprise me.'

Then he showed me a dark brown disc of bone.

'Can you tell what that is?' he demanded.

'No.'

'It is a knee-cap. From Saint Francis of Assisi himself.'

'Really?' I said.

'And this,' he told me, in hushed tones of reverence, 'is the nipple of Mary Magdalene.'

Yet, in all honesty, it did not look so – being hard, black, shrivelled and wrinkled, it looked more like a dried grape or olive-stone.

Then there was a withered finger, that without doubt had come from a human hand – which he said had been that of Osburh, mother of Good King Alfred of Wessex.

The final item he had to show me – an ochre lump – was dried dragon's blood, he said, of great value as a medicament. He told me the blood had been spilled when the dragon Ossula died on the tusks of his great enemy, Odun the Giant Elephant of Africa.

I observed that it was prescient of whoever first garnered these precious relics to think it important to collect the Virgin's milk, or the child Peter's foreskin, before their import to history could even be guessed.

'Yes,' he said, 'exactly so. It is these rare, fortunate, chance occurrences that make these relics so rare, so valuable, and so expensive to procure.'

When I told the dealer that I was no stranger to relics myself, and had once had in my possession both skulls of Saint Odo, he was not visibly impressed. But he asked me if I still had them, as he would be curious to see them for himself.

'Alas, no,' I said, 'for my wife threw them into a pond.'

He clucked his understanding. He remarked that I should not lament the loss too much. For, he said, Saint Odo was a minor, rarely collected, inexpensive saint, of the second or third rank, and that, when it came to bones in general, and the skull-trade in particular, there were many fakes, falsities and pretenders.

He warned me of passing-off, saying that some rascals raided grave-yards and butchers' bins to effect false relics, which they boiled in acid, cooked in ovens, or buried in lime, to achieve the impression of age and veracity.

He warned that I should only purchase from dealers of repute, like himself, of which there were only a handful in Christendom.

He went through his relics, saying how much a very rich man would have to pay for each. But he said that, as his friend, I might buy them cheaper.

Then I realised that he was not showing me his collection from pride, or a pleasure in possession, but to try to sell them. To me.

So I told him frankly I could not afford his prices.

He winced and gurned, pondered solemnly a moment, then smiled anew.

'Perhaps,' he said, 'you'd care to procure a pardon instead. Pardons offer salvation too. But often they come cheaper.'

'Pardons?' I said.

So he drew out of his pouch some small squares of vellum, rustling them, which he said were pardons, signed by divers Popes, or cardinals of the first rank, both living and dead, granting pardon and forgiveness for a range of sins.

'Let me see what I can offer you . . .' He sorted through the sheets. 'Here is a pardon,' he said, 'if you have had improper relations with your neighbour's wife . . .'

'Not me,' I said, 'I have never yet been offered that temptation.'

'Have you killed a member of the clergy but without intent?'

'No.'

'Cursed your master?'

'No,' I lied.

'Stolen a sheep, or livestock of similar value . . . such as two geese, three ducks or four chickens?'

'No.'

'Lied on a Sunday?'

'Not that either.' I deceived him again.

He looked at me with some dejection, as if I had exhausted all his trust in me.

'If you prefer,' he said, after some pause, 'I could sell you an indulgence instead.'

'An indulgence?'

'It is forgiveness for a sin you have yet to commit. It is better suited to those who prefer to sin sparely, at leisure, in moderation, and who care to plan ahead.'

'A pardon in advance?'

'Exactly so.'

I considered this. But it tasted dry on my palate.

'Doesn't that defeat the point?' I asked. 'There could be no guilty pleasure in it. For if I was already forgiven, I would not even feel I was committing a sin. And I would be left with nothing to regret . . .'

'I fear,' he said tartly, turning his back upon me, stuffing his pardons back into their leather sack, 'we are wasting each other's time . . .'

At dusk on the second day, we reached Franken Champney, and camped out around a large fire in the pasture behind the grave-yard.

The church was home of the Anchoress Agnes. Twenty-seven years before, at her request, the bishop had arranged the building of a small cell for her in the wall of the church, about four paces by three, and, after saying the Rites for the Dead, they had sealed the door to brick her in, and so bury her, that she might pass from the hurly-burly, hoopla and hullabaloo of this life into an after-life of calm seclusion, to pray for the world.

But, although she was buried alive, she was never cut off, for she had two small, slit windows. The one on the outside was just wide and deep enough to pass her food and drink in a bowl, and to receive a chamber-pot and anything else she wished to pass out. The smaller window on the inside wall of the church – the squint – allowed her to watch and hear the services within the church and praise the Lord with the congregation.

And in the roof of her cell there was a small gap in the

tiles, covered in sacking, which allowed sunlight, in mild moderation, to filter through.

Most times Agnes kept to herself and held her own counsel, or addressed herself directly to God. But sometimes she held brief muttered conversations with passers-by, through the slit window, and would enquire what month it was, and who had died, and what news there was from neighbouring villages. And occasionally she could be heard singing strange interminable songs, of her own devising, with odd, plaintive harmonies, peppered with new words of her own construction.

And just sometimes – when the Spirit moved her – she would scream odd warnings and strange instructions that those in earshot could not heed, for none could fathom them.

Anchoress Agnes was greatly honoured by the villagers. They fashioned small models of her for pilgrims to buy, made from clay, or carved from wood, with wild, straggly, white lamb's wool for hair, as lucky charms or protection against a range of ills – including warts, boils, headaches, infertility, itching, udder-fever in cows, imaginings and worry in people, swine-fever, distemper, and canker in dogs. In some of these statuettes Agnes was thin and tall, in others fat and bent, sweet-featured or scary. None could be judged as a faithful or false likeness. For Anchoress Agnes had not been seen clearly by man or dog for twenty-seven years. Only sometimes people thought they caught a glimpse, through the slit in the wall, of her eyes, reflecting back the light, like glistening brown buttons.

*

After we ate that night, I fell into a long conversation with Daniel, a scrivener, and we debated the pox and wondered on the Lord's intentions in visiting it on the world, and taking the lives of so many – the wicked and the innocent, rich and poor, man and woman, babes and crones.

Daniel told me how he had seen the Flagellants at Michaelmas at Saint Paul's in London. He told me how six hundred of these abject souls had come from Zealand in Flanders to do their penance to appease the Lord.

They wore caps with a red cross and would file, two by two, in a long column, singing hymns with their eyes cast down, then formed a circle and stripped to the waist, with their clothes piled up in the centre. And then they would commence to flog themselves and each other, wailing and howling terribly, loud enough to wake the dead. Each of them with a three-stranded whip with metal claw-tips. Tearing open their flesh, spraying blood all around them, spilling themselves on the unwary bystander, squirting themselves all over the ground.

And to join this Fraternity of the Cross you had to first pay for the privilege – four pennies a day for your food and lodgings.

And you made the promise to flog yourself three times each day for thirty-three days in succession – one day for each year of Jesus' life.

And for all this time you could not change your clothes, receive medicine or treatment, sleep in a bed, talk to the other sex, or wash your body. But first you must confess every sin you committed since the age of seven.

This way you could show the Lord you truly repented your full life-time of sin and so escape from a burning Hell.

But Daniel the scrivener had been unimpressed by the spectacle, and said how the passer-by would have to stop to clean the blood off from his discoloured shoes, and sometimes your hose or jacket got spattered too, said how the noise of it was horrible, how it made the children cry and scared the horses too. He remarked that if Flanders folk thought to flog themselves close to death, they should better stay home and do it in Flanders.

The Lord would not approve either, he said, for they were miserable sinners trying to cheat their deserved fate.

I thought back to my time as a scribe in the monastery, and how we would erase old writing from vellum by washing and scratching, so that it would come clean to be used again.

So I suggested to Daniel that perhaps this world was God's palimpsest. And that he was using the pox as his eraser, so he might clear large swathes of that clumsy, awkward, crossed, dotty, loopy, part-joined-up writing we call humankind. For the Lord had written for folk to be author of their own fate, with the choice to be good or bad, and we had, too often, chosen wrong.

So the Almighty had decided to rub us out and start over again.

Daniel said that this may be God's plan, for man had

163

defaulted on his contract with God, by disobeying his commandments too often, and building a Church in his name that was itself foul and corrupt.

I was surprised by this turn of the conversation. So I asked, 'Yes? How is the Church corrupt?'

And he must have considered all of this sometime before because he replied promptly, and with vehemence, without any pause for thought –

'Because it claims earthly powers it does not have, following the evil example of the Church of Rome.

'Because it ordains priests without basis in scripture or precedent.

'Because its leaders preach celibacy but are sodomites, defilers and lechers themselves.

'Because it is pure idolatry to claim that the communion wafer is the body of Christ.

'Because their rites and rituals are no more than acts of witchcraft.

'Because they extract bribes in return for prayers for the dead.

'Because they are uncharitable to the poor by denying them the same respect as the rich.

'Because they hawk pardons like cuts of cheese.

'Because they presume to forgive sins when only God has that power.

'Because they make false idols and graven images against the express command of God Almighty.

'Because they venture out on blasphemous crusades, bent on murdering our human brothers and sisters, when

164

God says we should forgive our enemies and befriend the stranger.'

'Oh,' I replied, 'because of *that* . . .' as if I had known all along. Then we sat in silence. And said no more about it. In truth, I had not heard anyone speak out against the Church before.

For, until Daniel the scrivener sewed this seed of doubt, I had trusted the Church as God's Own voice on Earth.

XVII. Wise Agnes in the Dark

I never presumed I'd get to visit the Anchoress Agnes myself, but as my fellow pilgrims fell to sleep, groaning, muttering and snoring, restless noisy as a pen of pigs, I found myself fretful, wide awake. So I stood up and paced about. Then it occurred to me I could wander up to see the famous cell of Agnes. I felt myself strangely drawn.

I trudged up the incline of pasture, over to the church, and along the path towards her stone mausoleum, built out of the side wall. I was curious to see this bricked-up prison. Perhaps I should say a prayer too.

The wind-twitched branches of a yew played shadows on the stones. An owl hooted at my approach. Something brisk and furry rustled the fallen leaves, scuttling between my splayed feet.

'You . . .' a voice sounded off. It was a shrill mix of words and a toothy, breathy whistle, punctuated by a wheeze. It came from the wall of the cell. The physician in me heard it as the raspy voice of a frail old woman with a weak, phlegmy chest, racking cough, and wide gaps in her teeth.

'Me?'

'You, darkly . . . in the bushes. Who . . . are you?'

'Jack Fox,' I said. 'I am a pilgrim. I come to pray, and to pay my respects.'

'Are you a living soul . . . or a dead soul?' she asked. She was not drunk, but she was slurred. She sounded all her s's as shhh's.

'Living?'

'Are you not a faerie, sprite or goblin?'

'I am not.'

'Do you have a solid body . . . of flesh?'

'I do.'

'Do you have wings too?'

'I do not.'

'Horns? Scales?'

'No.'

'Claws or a tail?'

'None of those.'

'Do you renounce the Evil One and all his works?'

'I do.'

'We must take care,' she said, hushing her voice to a whisper, to exclude other ears. 'By night, in this grave-yard all manner of damaged beings pass through. Fallen angels, demons, sprites, lost souls, ghosts, ghouls. Some are bod-ied, some are not. Some pretend to be things they are not. Some do not even know what they are. Some do not even know they are dead. Some come for help. Some to tempt me to sin or taunt me. Some have just lost their way . . .'

'They say you have visions,' I remarked.

'It is a gift. The Holy Family show themselves to me.'

'They do?'

'Our Lord Jesus Christ, many times. And his Mother Mary too.'

'That is a great blessing,' I said. 'And a rare privilege. What is it like?'

'There is dazzling, golden light, like the flare of a thousand candles, with wondrous smells, and music of great, great beauty. It is from the choirs of angels. My body shakes and I tumble to the ground. I tremble to the Lord. I am racked by deep spasms of joy. I howl with pleasure. I shudder with delight.'

'And then?'

'Our Lord Jesus speaks to me . . .'

'What does He say?'

'One time He asks, "Why do you abandon me, Agnes, when I have never abandoned you?"'

'Yes?'

'Another time He shows me a hazelnut in His palm and says, "Look, God loves you as much as this, for He loves everything the same. For all are equal in His Creation. The Pope, the leper, the louse and the hazelnut."'

'Oh,' I said.

'Then Jesus gave me the gifts of melancholy and tears, so I should have my own work, and might lament for mankind, and weep for the world, long and hard as my earthly work.'

'So, do you weep often?'

'Most hours of the day, these last twenty years.'

'Oh . . .' I said. I nodded my sympathy. 'That's a lot of sorrow, and many tears.'

I said that the world warranted tears now, with the pestilence abroad, killing almost everyone it touched, destroying families, villages and towns, spreading the stench of decay, turning people against each other, making us live in permanent fear.

I spoke of the lumps, the headaches, the fever, the coughing of blood, the blackened fingers and toes, the purple spots, the foul smell, the contortions of the sufferer's face . . . How it killed in hours or days. How no cure had been found.

She asked what treatments people had tried.

'Nigh well everything,' I said.

She asked how it carried from person to person.

I shrugged. 'On the wind, by sight, by smell, by touch . . .'

'Are there no bats, keeping company with this disease?'

'Not that I have seen.'

'Cats?'

'No.'

'Dogs?'

'No.'

'Donkeys?'

'Not that I've seen.'

'There must be rats, then?'

'Sometimes rats are near the disease. Sometimes the pestilence kills them.'

'Are there fleas?'

'Well, yes,' I said, 'of course. Where there are folk, there are always fleas.'

'What is the temper of the fleas? How do they act?'

'They are fierce. They are restless. They are jumpy.

They flee the sick to leap on the healthy.'

We considered this as a sudden gust of wind whistled through the yew.

'Perhaps,' she said, 'you should address the fleas. It seems the fleas know more than you.'

'Perhaps,' I said. But that's the trouble with mystics. Half the time they talk in riddles.

'Things will get worse, by and by,' she advised.

'They will?'

'Before they get better.'

'Oh . . .' I said.

'So you must learn to tell them apart . . .' she advised.

'Tell what apart?'

'The demon from the pig, and the pig from the man.'

'Yes?'

'But when all is lost, you will find salvation.'

'Good. Thank you for your good counsel,' I said.

'I wish you a good life,' she said, 'but you have held me from my melancholy . . . Now, I must go weep for the world afresh.'

I made the sign of the cross. I wished her well. I turned my back. I trudged away. I heard a quiet wailing commence behind me, but building in loudness as I walked away. Till shortly it became a full-blown howl.

I feared the worst. Then it came about.

The pestilence had come amongst us again. And it was Daniel the scrivener, and Jude the relic-seller, who first showed the signs of the curse – blackened tongues, frothy,

171

discoloured pee, a fierce fever, foul bodily smell, purpled swellings.

News spread quickly amongst our band of pilgrims, with shrieks and screams and howls, and folk fled in all directions, with eyes cast down, to prevent them seeing the evil, holding cloth to mouth, to prevent themselves breathing in the pox, holding their nostrils, so as not to smell the foul miasma.

So I promptly found myself alone by our dead fire with Daniel and Jude, tending them as best I could but with little hope of saving them.

Shortly, three burly, red-faced men came on horse-back.

'I am the lord's bailiff,' said one, scowling down at me. 'Who are you?'

I told them my name and occupation as scribe.

'And who are they?' he barked, gesturing to my sick, sprawled companions.

I gave their names too. I said they were a scrivener and a dealer in religious relics. I said they were good, decent people, on pilgrimage, but that they both shared the misfortune of being struck down by the pox.

They wheeled their horses away and trotted around us in a widening radius.

'And you?' said the bailiff. 'Do you not have the pox?'

'Not me,' I reassured them, 'it seems not to touch me. But it does always follow me, close behind, wherever I go . . .'

XVIII. The Pig's Tale

It's a barbed, twisty tale, tangled as bramble.

It is how I came to be arrested, accused of plotting, poisoning and heresy, and came to share the mean conditions of my confinement with another, who was a young spotted pig, with coarse bristles to his back, and black patches to his hams and wattles.

I shared a cell with this pig, with straw for bedding, slops for food, and two long days of tedium, awaiting my trial.

I take as I find. The pig was an amiable, good-natured companion. Though his manners were robust and his hygiene casual.

To follow the curlicues of the narrative, you'll have to first consider the ways of the pox – how it travelled invisibly, arriving without warning, striking with ferocity, killing almost all it touched.

I strained to understand my captors' view of it. With no knowledge of the plague's source, or where it would strike next, or why, there arose a fear of human subterfuge, that people were poisoning the water, or spoiling the food, or fouling the air. Then suspicions fell on strangers, travellers and outsiders – those beyond the social pack, in particular –

i. Vagrants, musicians, dancers and foreigners.

ii. Demons, the un-alive and un-dead.

iii. Lepers, whores and tricksters.

iv. Gypsies and tumblers.

v. Dark-skinned people.

vi. Jews in disguise.

vii. Heretics.

So in Fenny Barton, with the pox breaking to the east in Little Stratford, and to the west in Great Hampney, and to the south in Rawstone, the villagers felt surrounded and became fearful for their own safety. So the lord of the manor, seeking to combat any human mischief in the spread of the pestilence, had instructed his bailiff, the steward and the almoner to locate any strangers or miscreants, and to treat them with suspicion, allow them no entry to the town, award them no kindness, and imprison them if they thought it best.

There are four stone-walled, iron-barred cells in the town's gaol. Two either side of a central pathway. You can see those opposite but they are too far away to reach an extended arm through the bars.

I immediately fall foul of Martin the gaoler through my poverty. For I find I am not only to be held against my will, but that I am expected to pay for the privilege a delivery fee of two whole shillings, and contribute to the cost of candles, my bedding and beer, and victuals for my captors.

'But I have no money,' I say. I spread my open, empty palms. For the small funds I have are banked privately within my person, where I hold them for extreme and terminal need.

'Then you will have to board with the paupers . . .' He spits.

He puts a hard hand in the small of my back and propels me into the large, straw-strewn cell, empty of any furniture or bedding.

There is one other pauper, already there.

He is the young, spotted boar. At first he seems alarmed by my presence, retreating to a corner, snorting disgruntled. But shortly, while never meeting my eyes, he sidles out sideways, as if by accident, until he is close enough to sniff at my leggings. And, finding me harmless, maybe palatable, gently chews on the toe of my boot.

'Oink,' say I.

'Honk,' says he. Or some such similar, slithery, hungry-sounding and dripping spittle. And brings his damp, pink, flat snout close to my face, to sample my scent. Then he moves alongside and suffers me to pat his firm, bristly back.

In the cell opposite is the man I knew before, from our earlier encounters, as Simon Mostly, only further damaged by bruising to his face. And he seems to have forfeited the tip of his nose, which is now reduced to an upturned crimson nub. And instead of two small nostrils and a divide, he has one larger, gaping hole.

In the cell alongside Simon is a masked man in sackcloth, who wears a bell on cord around his neck, signalling his movements, who I take to be a leper.

Leprosy is not an easy scourge to comprehend. Some say it is a stain. That the leper has been marked out by God's displeasure to wear lascivious sin upon the skin. Others insist that lepers are souls bound for Heaven, no better nor worse than us, but suffering their Purgatory in this earthly life, rather than after death.

Some say that leprosy is simply a disease, not a state of moral impurity. But it is a disease that can be spread by touch or intimacy.

For this reason the leper must live outside the village or town. And the Church makes rules for him –

   i. Always shout 'Unclean! Unclean!' wherever you go.
   ii. Never enter a church, market, inn or any public place.
  iii. Wear a mask, ring a bell, and keep your lips covered.
  iv. Never wash in public water.
   v. Never touch a child.
  vi. Never enter a narrow lane.
 vii. Never speak a word up-wind of the healthy.
viii. Never eat or drink with anyone save fellow lepers.

Simon Mostly says that the leper is called Lumpy John and belongs to him. He says he has bought him from an Irish horse-trader for the price of a donkey and seven shillings.

I ask him why he came to agree this purchase when you can ride a donkey all day, while a leper can never carry you half so far, and when so many other people choose to shun lepers like the plague, for fear of contagion.

Simon says that, well cared for and well used, a leper can earn a handsome keep for himself and his master, through spiritual service.

He says that if I give him only three pennies he will let me kiss his leper.

'Kiss him?' I enquire.

'Or lick him, for four pennies, if you prefer, which is an opportunity denied to most.'

'Yes?' I ask. 'To whose benefit?'

'Indeed, it will help *you*,' he says. 'For it will signal to God Almighty your penitence and humility, and that you throw yourself open to His will, even to the extent of risking contracting leprosy yourself.'

'Yes?'

'And what nobler example can a man follow than that of Our Lord Jesus, who, it is told in the Gospel of Luke, reached out to touch lepers, and so cured ten on His way to Jerusalem, though only one ever returned to thank Him.'

'That's so,' I remember. 'Exactly so.'

'And think too of the Gospel of Matthew, and how Jesus came down after the Sermon on the Mount, and a leper came and said, "Make me clean," and Our Lord reached out and touched him, and cured him instantly.'

'Yes,' I agree, 'it would be a fine thing to kiss your leper for myself . . . But, at present, I do not have the pennies to fund that ambition. And, as things have it, he is locked away, *there*, beyond reach . . .'

*

Then, to pass the time, Simon began to tell me what he'd learned of the pig, my companion behind bars.

He said that a man known as Richard Bacon had been arrested in Stoke Charnley by the sergeant of the manor, on suspicion of spreading the pox by poisoning wells. But as it was late and a storm was raging, they rested overnight, locking Richard Bacon in a secure barn, chained to a ring in the wall. But in the morning he was nowhere to be seen. And in his place was the young spotted boar. Nonchalant and cock-sure as you like.

At first it was supposed that the prisoner had escaped. But a search of the barn found it entirely sound and secure, with no gap, hole, or possible exit. And in the centre of the floor lay Bacon's clothes, strewn here and there, quite emptied of their owner.

So then they understood. They supposed that Bacon, with magics and Satanic aid, must have transformed himself into a pig, to confuse or mock his persecutors. And that it was a deliberate provocation and crude pun upon his name. For, in reverse of the usual course of events, Bacon had turned into a pig.

And it was in this unchanged, porcine state that Richard Bacon was still being held. And folk said he showed his arrogant contempt for his captors, and fellow defendants. For he shat and pissed wherever, whenever the mood took him. Frothed at the mouth with excitement. Snorted rudely. And sometimes fell asleep, snuffling and snoring loudly, in complete disregard of the solemn proceedings, while appearing before his accusers and betters.

For my part, I was never convinced that the pig was a philosopher in disguise, or otherwise possessed of a demon.

I believed there was a mistake in identity. The pig was most likely a pig.

There is no sure, established scientific method for rooting out if the soul of a man has taken its possession of the body of a pig, but Brother Fulco had always taught me the power of evidence. So I observed my cell-mate as fairly and scrupulously as I could.

Richard Bacon, I was told, was a former monk, an all-chemist and astrologer.

If so, he would surely know Latin. He would speak some Greek. He would be cognisant of algebra, and conversant with the physics. He might well be familiar with German too.

So, I tried testing his understanding of various tongues.

'*Alles hat ein Ende, nur die Wurst hat zwei,*' I said.

But no sign of recognition played on his sly, porky face. I got no more in response than a casual grunt.

'*Sus magis in coeno gaudet, quam fonte sereno,*' I said, but detected no sign of understanding. He just raised a leg and languidly passed water in a spreading, frothy, yellow puddle.

Then, I tried being sly, and sought to surprise him, with unexpected riddles. Then, I would sidle close to his side and whisper to his ear –

> 'I have a heart that never beats,
> I have a home but I never sleep.

179

I can take a man's house and build another's,
And I love to play games with my many brothers.
I am a king among fools.
Who am I?'

And, when that failed to evoke any interest, I tried the simpler conundrum –

'Say my name and I disappear.
What am I?'

But, if he knew, he wasn't saying. Or maybe that was just his subtle way of answering truly.

I understood the proper concerns of the court. If the animal was possessed of the malignant soul of a man, or some demonic force, he must be thwarted and the possession must be exposed.

And even if the pig was just a pig, it still could not go unpunished.

For if the demons saw that animals could evade the sanctions of a proper trial and retribution, they would surely start occupying animals the more often, to perpetrate their evil work, knowing they would escape unchallenged, unpunished.

It would not be fair for the farmer, small-holder, or the beasts themselves, to make the everyday animals of the field empty vessels for Satan, to be the shell of his demons.

If the maleficence of one pig was allowed, all pigs would be at greater jeopardy. A moral pollution would surely spread. And then all animals would come under greater threat of possession – cows, chickens, ducks, goats and sheep. Once the possession was allowed to pass unpunished, the very ground would be tainted and tarnished, for those devils and demons would claim squatters' rights, then tenure, and thereinafter could only be expelled by exorcism. Thus any acts of criminality, or offence against the Lord, committed by animals, had to be ruthlessly prosecuted, for the protection of us all. Which was why the infamous Cockerel of Baden-Baden had been throttled for laying an egg, in defiance of his God-given masculinity and the natural division of the sexes, consequent on some intercourse he'd had with a demon, from which the offspring would surely have been a sinister cockatrice.

And a hive of bees were smothered for stinging to death their keeper.

And a sow that had killed a child was hanged, along with her litter – for all the piglets had just watched the slaughter of the infant without intervention, complaint or comment.

Yet there was mercy. For others were acquitted. Like the she-ass who was caught *in flagrante delicto*, in an act of coition with her keeper. For many witnesses came forward to speak of her good character and said she was a demure and modest ass, more sinned against than sinning.

Then there was a flock of starlings who were called to appear before the court to answer to eating a field of barley. But, though they never came to face the charge, their attorney gained them full pardon, arguing they could not be expected to make the journey, given a fear of being attacked by birds of prey on the way.

XIX. Telling Stories

I grasp your conjecture.

You suppose that since I have written this story down, years after the events described, I have survived my incarceration and imminent trial, and emerged from this jeopardy unscathed, to sit here, now, before this roaring fire, at my oak desk, scratching my mature and ample rump, perhaps with a jug of mulled Frenchy wine at my elbow, with a plate of piquant, roasted crow giblets to snack upon, with a goose-feather quill to dip into my marble ink-well, to scrawl on the finest parchment, a penny a sheet, maybe having become a mature man of wealth who has fared well in life, being favoured for his good looks, and rewarded for his talents and labours, perhaps fathering seven children, while outliving four wives.

And you may think that because I write of myself as the hero of my own story, I must have a high regard for myself, to place myself alongside other protagonists of literature such as Saints, Apostles, Prophets, Pharaohs of Egypt, Monsters, Angels, Cannibals and Monarchs, just because I have become well known for my skills at physic, and as a purveyor of poultices, and the author of two celebrated texts on medicine, respected master of four domestic servants, and elected member of the Guild of Surgeons, welcomed as friend to the homes of well-known nobles.

But I must tell you now that nothing is so simple, for this story-telling opens up a sackful of frogs, all leaping out in their different directions, while croaking discordant.

You would not believe the armies of people involved in any tale. Nor the profusion of occasions that arise in any story.

For a start, the me *now* is not the me *then*. And the me that writes this down is not the me he observes, for the *see-er* and the *seen* have to stand apart and separate, with different perspectives. And, besides these two wastrels, tied up in past times, in the labyrinth of stories, is another *me*, as I live and breathe, who goes about his everyday tasks, and has no truck with gossiping on shadows. In fact, he despises the wasted effort and idle supposition.

And, forgive me for saying, there are at least two of you. For the *you* I suppose as my reader cannot be the *you* you are. For everyone is different some ways from everyone else. Yet I cannot write a separate narrative for each and every one of you, to match your peculiarities, for vellum is too pricey, and ink would run dry, and eternity would come to an end.

So I have made some polite surmises regarding your character, that I may guess what you care to hear.

I have supposed you like visiting other people's business, and hearing their intimate thoughts, peering under their beds, and knowing their most private moments, all the while condemning them religiously for their flaws and sins, perhaps figuring yourself their moral superior. But, perhaps I have judged you wrong.

184

Then, when it comes to time, we are hopeless tangled. For there must be a long succession of *thens*, as the sequence of events in the story, each with a *later-on* when their effects find fruition, and a string of *after-thats* as I write it all down, followed by that string of *nows*, including this one, now just gone, linked but separate, like a string of beads, as you read it. Never mind the endless *what-ifs* that we can only guess at. So soon you have as many parallel lines of time as furrows in a newly ploughed field. So you are trudging up and down, down and up, pulling a dead weight, like a team of oxen, through the stony ground of the reader's indifference.

So I ask you politely. Bear with me. For this is no easy task. Pray don't jump to any hasty conclusions. There is a deal of ploughing still to come. And boulders to be cleared by hand.

I saw matters were coming to a head when the sergeant bundled in with two other burly fellows to dress Richard Bacon, the pig, in human clothes – collared shirt, red woollen jerkin with wood toggle-buttons, breeches that reached past his hocks, and leather boots.

It was a struggle for all, with wrestling about in the straw, biting, blows, tugging of ears, squealing, threats, snorts and curses. For the pig preferred to stay naked, seeing the clothes as an affront to his candour, an imposition upon his will, an encumbrance to his freedoms, while the sergeant insisted he be clothed. Not cower behind the hide of a pig, but stand trial as a man.

They wanted him to be dressed so he could enact what they supposed him to be. A wilful human, masquerading in a beast's body. And, in his full attire, still squealing in protest, he was led away, with a rope around his lace-collared neck, leaving me alone in the pauper's cell.

But it is not long before I too receive a visitor. He is a tall, thin-faced man with a staring expression that couples a wince with a smile. He says he is my attorney. Paid for by the public purse. And that he'll represent my cause in court so justice can be done.

'Court?' I say.

'The assize,' he says, 'today. Presently. To answer to a judge and jury. But mostly to God.'

'The charges against me?'

He unrolls a sheet of vellum and starts to read. 'Witch-craft and diabolism . . . intoxicating . . . bewitching and poisoning.'

'Truly?' I frown. 'Surely not . . . me?'

He holds a finger to his lips, to silence me, to convey that he is not finished yet. 'Imprisoning spirits against their will . . . Entrapping the soul of a man in the body of a pig . . . Conspiring with said pig . . . Poisoning the wells and waters to spread the Great Pestilence.'

We consider this in silence for some moments.

'If you are to be my attorney,' I say, 'what do you advise?'

He thinks an instant, then issues a quicksilver smile. 'It is certainly better to hang than to burn,' he says.

'Meaning?'

'I can plead for you. If you admit to the poisoning but deny the witchcraft, you will earn some credit for honesty. The court may believe you. Then you may earn a kinder end.'

'And if I am to plead innocent of all these charges? For I am innocent.'

He shakes his weary head. His dull grey eyes, with their pink whites, avoid mine, staring past my shoulder. 'Then I cannot save you. For the evidence against you is awful strong.'

'Evidence?' I say.

'The jury are twelve good men and true. Fair-minded and self-informing,' he says. 'They have investigated the case already and discussed it in every small aspect. I have talked with them. No one speaks a good word for you. I believe they will surely convict. I think they mean for you to burn.'

When I appear before the court, I am led out with my hands bound, as though I am already a guilty man. The steward and a priest sit behind a raised desk. To the side sits the jury of twelve good men and true. They are surly and unfriendly to a man, and return my smiles with stubborn glares.

Then a scowling attorney begins to harangue me with questions, posed in hostile and suspicious terms, seeking to contrive the most damning construction on my conduct.

Question: Is your occupation that of a witch, necromancer and diabolist?
Answer: No.

Question: Are you in league with the Devil? Do you not conspire with Lucifer, Satan or his lesser demons?
Answer: I do not. I would not. I never have.

Question: Have you not entrapped the soul of a man within the body of a pig, and engaged in other demonic transformations?
Answer: No, I have not. Not once. Never.

Question: Are you not yourself a demon, hiding in a man's body, behind the manners of a fool?
Answer: No, sir. I am not. I swear it.

Question: Do you travel with a black cat as your familiar?
Answer: Cats? No, sir. I do not travel with them. Not me.

Question: Do you not travel this land bringing the Great Pestilence in your wake, visiting it upon those you meet?
Answer: It is true I have been unlucky in this regard. For wherever I go, the pestilence follows. So far, I have lost thirty-two brothers in Christ, a wife, three ladies of the bed-chamber, and two fellow pilgrims to this Great Mortality, the pox.

Question: Do you not spread the pestilence by poisoning the wells and the foods?
Answer: I do not, sir. I do not know why the pestilence persists in dogging my steps so closely.

Question: It always follows you?
*Answer: Yes. Wherever I go, it appears two or three days
behind me.*

*Question: Do I hear you right? Are you now threatening us,
here gathered?*
*Answer: No, sir. I am not. I wish you the best of health. But
I cannot speak for the pox, which has a will of its own.*

The attorney asks me to account for my past movements. So I tell him truthfully –

I was a novice in the monastery at Whye until the Black
Death killed all my brother monks.

I stayed at Coppetts Pond in the woods until the pestilence came and killed my companion.

I took myself to the inn at Ravenstone until the Great
Mortality struck there too, killing half the village.

I moved on to Franken Champney, but the pestilence
followed me there.

I am gladdened to see Simon Mostly called as witness. He
is a friend. He knows me well and can attest to my good
character.

But, having sworn on the Bible, to tell the truth and
nothing but the truth, may God Almighty strike him
down if he lies, he declares that he has seen myself and the
said pig, in the cell opposite, converse in our intrigue. He
declares we turned our backs on the company, and whispered to avoid being overheard, and sometimes spoke the
Latin to avoid being understood. Nonetheless, he heard

us talk clearly of the poisoning of waters, and the fouling of wells.

Further, he says that I, not the pig, was the leading actor in this complot.

He says he knows me from before, and that I carry skulls as demonic ornaments, and wherever I go the pestilence shortly follows, and that I am spreading death as an agent of Lucifer himself.

He testifies that I am a heretic and preach for sin and the Devil. He claims I said that Lucifer was as great as God, for there could not be one without the other. For there could be no high without low, light without dark, good without evil.

Further, Simon says that I am always speaking out against my betters. He tells the court that I said the lord of the manor was like a leech or scavenger, for he sucks the blood of the sick, harvests what he never grew, and steals the labour of others, as if it is his own.

Tears well, to trickle down Simon's cheeks as he points to me as Devil Incarnate. He crosses himself. He weeps. He sniffs. He snuffles. He rubs his tearful, bloodshot eyes. He begs the court and the Church for their protection, to save him from the malice of my vengeance.

I can see clearly from the scowls and stares of the jury, and the unblinking, unkind look of the judge, that the trial is not proceeding to my advantage.

XX. Poxed

It is a harsh truth to learn you must burn. But we all must die. In the fullness of our tenure on flesh, before our lease on life is run. And the secret is to die well. Confessed. Penitent. Absolved. Embracing the bigger, better, eternal life to come.

For we all must pay a price. None of us is innocent, however we plead. We are all guilty – imperfect, fallen fledglings who must be helped to penitence and to rise again.

If I am given the choice to burn briefly on a bonfire in Franken Champney, or for all eternity in the Pits of Hell, I know which I will choose. Besides, Brother Falco once told me, there's a knack to being burned alive. If you can only swallow your tongue, you pass away from a dearth of breath before the flames can ever reach you. Which spares much pain.

That is the beauty and indestructibility of truth. It is why we should never spurn any single grain of knowledge on the beach of wisdom. You may learn something. And it lies like a seed, dormant in your mind for twenty years. Until you find its use.

All the same, I addressed myself to the Almighty. I prayed that He might find a use for me in His Divine plan. And that plan had me alive, not dead.

I reminded Him I was young, with the hope of a long span ahead. I said I would pledge my life to His service. And give myself, like Saint Odo, to the harvesting of knowledge and the service of the sick. All that afternoon we heard the distant screams and squeals of the pig.

You could hear that they were beating him and using spikes, screws and other metallic persuasions.

And when he was returned to the gaol at dusk, we saw he had been horribly used, terribly man-handled. They had torn the shirt from him, and all along his back were deep, weeping ridges where he had been struck by some long hard rod. He was gone lame in his rear legs, dragging his hind end, belly to the ground. He was bleeding from his nose and ears.

In the cell he lay panting on his side, eyes half-open but glazed, unseeing.

I could see what had passed. They had tried to make him talk. They had tried to force him to recognise the court. They had sought to drive any demons out. But, despite their blows and threats and contraptions, it was all in vain.

Man or pig, it was a terrible, ugly way to treat a member of Creation.

Martin, the warder, comes to the bars of my cage to talk to me.

'They will burn you in the morning,' he says. 'You. And the pig too.'

'I know,' I say, 'can you call a priest? I must confess. I need absolution before I go beyond.'

He purses his lips. He considers. 'If you have any valuables hidden, you should show me now. For you surely cannot take them with you. And it would be a shame to have then burn.'

'I have nothing,' I say.

For, in truth, all I have left to give back to the world are some words of warning to the sinful, besides the Abbot's ring and a single gold coin, lodged up my arse.

'Because if you paid me,' Martin slurs, 'I could get you a priest. Some food too. And I could give you a draught before they take you.'

'A draught?'

'Hemlock and opium poppy in spirit. So you would not feel any pain.'

I see the bubbles of sweat on his forehead. I smell his rotten, sulphur breath. I see the acorn swelling in his neck.

'Are you well, Brother Martin?' I ask.

'I am dizzy,' he says. And he sways away, then back, as if addled by ale.

'I am a surgeon,' I say, 'I think I know what ails you. It's clear to see.'

'What is that?'

'I must examine you,' I say, 'to be sure. You must place your hand between the bars.'

I press my fingers to his wrist. He is burning hot. His heart is racing. It is a stallion at full gallop.

'You must sit here by the bars, and lean towards me,' I say. 'I must reach under your arms.'

'Yes?' he says. 'What can you feel?'

'One lump . . . two lumps . . . three lumps . . .' I say. 'And a black rash on your chest.'

'Is that bad?'

'It's not good.'

'Is there a name for it?' he asks.

'There is,' I say. 'I know several.'

'Tell me.'

'The Curse, the Pox, the Pestilence, the Great Mortality, the Blue Death . . .'

'Will I live?' he moans.

'It is not unknown,' I console, 'but it's very rare.'

'I cannot stand,' he sighs. 'My head is on fire. My legs have melted.'

He is slumped on the floor, against the bottom bars of my cell, pushing down with his hands on the flag-stones, trying to raise himself up.

'You must rest first,' I say, 'to regain some strength.'

On the right side of his belt, nearest to me, he has a bone-handled knife in its leather sheath. On the further side, on a large brass ring, hang the four keys to the four separate cells.

I know. Nothing in God's Kingdom happens by chance. The Lord does not play dice. Either He wills it to happen, or He gives us the mind to choose.

So, I fall to my knees. I pray.

My Saviour has reached down to protect me again.

I thank Him for my imminent freedom, for my escape from burning, for the beauty of the world, for the friendship and love I had received, for the breeze through the

194

willows on a summer day, for the taste of honey, for the touch of Cecilia, for everything, for all.

I pray for the soul of the pig. All in all, he is a good pig. He is an open and friendly character, and carries himself well. I pray he be absolved of his sins. I pray for Simon Mostly, too, that he find some way to shed his mountain of guilt, to repent and be saved. Then I scrabble on all fours and reach through the bars to unhook the keys from the warder's belt.

'Don't . . .' he groans. 'Leave it . . .' He waves weakly with his hand, like a drunk trying to swat a fly.

'Will you stop me, then?' I ask. But he doesn't raise his arm to me, for he no longer has the strength.

Simon Mostly watches me turn the key in the lock and swing open the creaking, rusted gate. He rushes forward, rattling the bars of his own cell. 'Release me too,' he says. 'My friend.'

'If I release you, friend,' I say, 'it will be unkind. They'll think you and I are plotters together, in league with the pig. You will not be safe from their wrath.' And so, with sadness, and to protect him, I turn my back.

But I open Lumpy John's cell. For he has hobbled to the bars, tugging at them, in his eagerness to be free. And I watch him stumble out silently, without a word or a backward look.

'Wait,' I call.

'Yes, my friend?' He turns. I expected to hear some guttural grunt or groan. But to my surprise he has a calm, resonant voice of beauty and clarity.

'I will kiss you, if I may.' And so I do, on the nubbly, corky bark of his cheek.

Then I steal a lick too. For good measure. And feel the better for it, though he is dry and salty with the hard, ridged texture of an oak trunk.

'Bless you, Brother,' he says, wiping the moisture from his cheek with the inside of his wrist.

And then he is gone, melted into the dark. God knows where.

I find courage.

Men may want me dead. But God decides to keep me alive.

I am hunted and must hide. Now I am a fugitive, outside the law. I need to be away from this place where people know my face. Anywhere else will do.

Away from here, I am anyone and no one, now. For nobody knows me. There is no one left to tether me to my past, or to call me by my name.

I can choose myself a title, and devise myself a history.

This time, I'll travel south.

I cannot out-run the plague. I know that now. Instead I will go where it has been already, where it has sated its terrible appetite, and eaten its fill.

I will hide where it has looked already.

Then I can see the chance for repair and renewal. Not watch the plague strike all over again.

XXI. The World Is Broke Apart

Everywhere the pestilence has broken things apart, churning the whole into shattered shards, and strewing the wreckage in its wake.

The old order is lost. Custom is torn apart. So many are dead. Everyone's lost someone close. We are all mourning now.

They used to bury folk one by one, with a head-stone, until the pox. Now they bury them by the dozens, in unmarked pits.

But what man digs under, the beasts dig up. So you come across a careless scatter of once-human parts and pieces – a leg here, a rib-cage there, a gnawed skull, a length of bowel – by the side of the road, in a ditch, by the river-bank.

So many broken hearts. So many villages lie empty, abandoned.

When it blows from the south, there is a putrid, rotten smell in the air.

Doors swing to and fro in the wind. Shutters hang off their hinges. Roofs have tumbled in. Fences are broken. Bridges are collapsed. Roads are rutted and pot-holed.

Crops lie unharvested, flattened, mushy, musty, blackened, rotting in the fields.

Farm animals are gone feral. They do not answer to a

human call. They flee from our sight. They wander where they will.

Dogs are gone wild and hunt in packs. They sense your mood. They can smell weakness. Carry a stick. Take care not to show them fear. You'd best consider them wolves.

Strangers pass by on the other side. You both look away. You stay silent.

So many emptied beds.

Most of the clergy lost, for they caught the plague, attending the dying.

And half the doctors are gone, too. Dead from keeping the company of the pox. Or else they fled.

Now kindness is discarded. It is a weak, broken utensil. It has no use in these hard times.

Faith is scoffed at. When the plague took the priests and babes, the holy, the best and the innocent – while the bad were saved – then belief was become the pastime of fools.

Authority is shamed. The King cannot command the plague. The clergy cannot explain it. The doctors cannot cure it. Arms cannot repel its attack.

The law is lost. Robbery is rife. Thieves and thugs go unpunished. Rogues rule the roads.

I walk all night, through the day into the following darkness.

I seek out the deep of the wood. I will be out of reach and recognition from my tormentors. I want distance and isolation. And I will know when I have found it.

I will be alone. I will hide my head. I will consider my choices. I will pray. I lament the errors of my ways.

198

As I trudge on, I take time to remember it all. I count back. I tally my unconfessed, unrepented, undischarged venial sins – lust, gluttony, greed, simony, sloth, wrath, envy, pride.

And then there are the grave matters, mortal sins, committed in full knowledge of their awfulness, with deliberation and consent.

I did not mention them before. For I cannot detain you with every last thing I did. But they are serious things, and better not shown naked in plain sight.

◆𒀭ℋ◆ ☉■♎ ◆𒀭☉◆	just the one time
◆𒀭ℳ □◆𒀭ℳ□	too many times to count
◆◆□□◆ℳ ◆□ℋ●●	often with several
◆𒀭ℳ ◆■◆□ℳ☉&☉♌●ℳ	twice
ℋ ⚡□□ꝏℳ◆ ℋ◆◆ ■☉○ℳ	a big number
⚡ ❖ℳ□⌧ ♌☉♎ ◆𒀭ℋ■ꝏ	seven times
☉ ●☉◆ꟽℋ❖ℋ□◆◆ □□☉ ꟽ◆ℋ◆ℳ	twice, but never on a Sunday

Yes, all that and –

◆𒀭ℳ ◆■○ℳ■◆ℋ□■☉♌● too.

In *The Great Unhappened*, Odo wrote of the far future time of the Buttoned People, when every soul's worth would be weighed not at Final Judgement, but every hour of every day.

For under the skin of every baby at birth was placed a small magic button. And it would send silent, invisible messages, quick as thought, all around to those boxes called Button-Readers. And these Readers were all-knowing. For the buttons were all-telling. They would tell who the person was, who their parents had been, what age they were, what illnesses they had, if they were educated, if they should be allowed to enter this place or another, if they had a licence to be intimate with others, what wrongs they had done in their life, small and major, and the state of their four humours, and the taints of their bodily fluids, and the flow of their bloods, and the foods they should eat, if they were allowed to wear an ermine collar, if they had a special title like Serf, Lord, Sir, Cow-Maid or Chancellor, whether they should curtsy to a duchess, or a bishop should bow to them, and the rewards they deserved, or the punishments they should suffer, everything being placed in the balance.

For, all around in the air, flew tiny machines called Fly-Eyes and Gnat-Ears and Bee-Noses, which could see and hear and smell all that happened around them, even in the dark. So they knew if a person had missed church on a Sunday, or slept with a neighbour's spouse, or spoken ill of a land-owner, or poached a deer, or passed wind, or partaken of some forbidden herb, or spoken a heresy, or worse.

And by their sins and goodness, and their rank at birth, people were allowed the wealth to buy what they needed, besides feathers for their hats, fur trim for their jerkins, and gold twine for their hose.

Now no coins changed hands. For money was no more. And instead there was only the tally of their goodness and their sins, and their worth as well-born or peasant.

*

I felt myself safer in the woods, where I could slink behind the trunk of a tree, drop behind a bush, melt into the shadows, where I might hear any approaching foot from the crunch of fallen leaves and the snap of broken twigs.

Perhaps I went feral.

The first week I did not build a fire, for fear of drawing attention to myself.

Each night I would find myself some fresh dip or hollow, lay branches over and cover them with ferns or foliage, then sleep beneath.

I lived like an animal. I grunted to myself. I sniffed the air to scent strangers or some distant fire. I crouched on all fours, and lapped water from puddles. I caught small beasts and chewed them raw, blood-warm, fur and all, crunching their bones, with the squirts of their juices bursting in my mouth.

I harvested the edible plants I could find – lovage, wild garlic, nettles, dandelion, wood-sorrel, chicory, harebell, red clover, creeping Charlie, elderberry. I gathered fungi and mushrooms too. The spotted redcap and the wizard's puffball which played tingling, teasing, scented games with my sight, gave sounds to the touch, and awarded an angelic halo to every blade of grass, and made the tree branches melt into the sky. It made the trunks breathe as they changed colour, while the ground shimmered and rippled like water, as the squirrels tumbled somersaults, and the crows sang '*Agnus Dei*', while the Earth spun like a top, till I passed out dizzied.

One sober supper-time, I paused in mid-bite. For I saw a strange sight reflected back to me in the dead rabbit's glistening eye. It was the image of a man, curved across the slick, amber, shiny eye-ball. But I did not recognise myself at first. I twisted the rabbit carcass to view my other cheek in its other eye. Then I drew this mirror closer.

I was gone. The person I was had left. Someone had replaced me.

The boy I used to be had fled my face, and never said goodbye.

I had a thick stubble on my cheeks and chin. I looked older, with a coarser skin and worry-lines to my eyes. My hair was a thick golden thatch. My lips were swollen plump. My eyes of duck-egg blue were evasive and inquisitive. Their view was shrewd and calculating. But I would not flatter them to call them kind.

Perhaps I was handsome, but it is not in my nature to be vain.

Time slows when you are alone in the forest, waiting for night to fall, and then for dawn, and then for dusk, and then for the same, all over again. Your mind strains to busy itself. You find solace in slow, unusual, solitary pastimes.

I counted back, trying to remember every last soul I had met in my life.

I named to myself all the cats I had known. And all the dogs too.

I recited to myself all that I could remember of Odo's great *Book of Life*.

I played chess in my head, against an imaginary opponent, but he always proved of identical strength, with the result that we always drew. He always saw the traps I laid for him, as I saw his coming, too.

It was not long before the rank smell of my own body took to offending my very own nose. So I started daily to bathe myself naked, kneeling in the chilly water of a stream.

I saw the flea-bites – white-headed, reddened pimples – scattered all over my chest and limbs.

So I hunted every last flea from my body, and deposited them unharmed on God's earth a hundred paces from my lair. I wished the beasties no harm or hurt. But I had suffered their random bites long enough.

So I wished them good health elsewhere, and to feel free to secure another habitation. The first day I found nineteen. The second day there were four. The third day there was one. And the fourth day there were none.

Perhaps I had needed rest. Maybe the medicine helped too. For I chewed on hemlock, rosemary and henbane leaves. And sucked on juniper berries.

I felt myself grow stronger and steadier. The lingering fever went. The headaches stopped too.

Those lumps that had come and gone in my groin and neck were evident no more.

One morning I woke in my leafy bed and found myself visited by a large warty toad, the width and breadth of my hand. It sat on its fat haunches, close to the side of my head, and observed me with unblinking amber eyes.

It must have been the ugliest, lumpiest, wartiest being I had ever witnessed. It would make a carbuncle look handsome. But it issued such a feeling of calm and good-will that I was moved to address it.

'Hello, warty brother,' said I. 'Well met . . .'

It nodded briefly. Then opened its mouth wide to croak something guttural.

I knew it spoke itself kindly and friendly. But I could not understand precisely what was said, for it spoke entirely in the croaky, slithery tongue peculiar and private to toads.

'Who are you? What do you want?' I enquired. 'Show me a sign.'

It was then that the full revelation occurred.

A brother toad – identical in its size, appearance and serene manner – hopped from nowhere to appear at its side. And the two of them squatted on their fat haunches, unblinking, regarding me calmly.

'Are you a manifestation?' I asked. 'An epiphany?'

They turned to eye each other. Then, nodding their agreement, they turned back to me and voiced themselves in unison.

'*Krrrrrk*,' they said. They said it in a single voice. They said it both together.

It was then I discerned their identity. I realised it all of a sudden. From their sublime ugliness, the grace of their spirit, the duality of their being, and the synchrony of their motions.

They had come to visit me in my solitary misery. They were come to save me from my slough of despair.

'Have no fear,' their presence said. 'You are not alone. You are never alone or forgotten. You are always in the Lord's sight. Jesus loves you. He loves you as much as an angel or a hazelnut. And so do we.'

'Do you carry a message?'

'*Krrrrk*,' they agreed.

'That it's safe to return?'

'*Krrrrk*,' one said.

'So, they've stopped looking for me?'

'*Krrrrk*,' observed the other.

Then, without a backward look, bounding into the ferns, they were gone. The two moving as one, as if to a single, gracious, generous mind.

Praise be to God.

The spirits of Saint Odo and Saint Odo, of Here and There, patron of the despised, homeless and helpless, reveal themselves in many forms. They bring comfort to the homeless, the helpless, those outcast and despised. They bestow their grace and favour, and move amongst us still.

So I knew it was time. To come out of the wilderness, where I had been for forty-odd days.

XXII. *The Return*

A column of grey smoke drifts from the chimney of the long house of the monastery. My feet are sodden, sucked by mud and cowpats.

There are three figures working in the garden. As I draw closer I recognise Huw from his stoop, and Matthew with his splay-footed limp, alongside another brother I do not know.

They pause in their labours and turn to look my way, but without any smile of recognition.

'Welcome, stranger,' says Huw, standing up, resting on his hoe. 'May God go with you.'

'Brother Huw,' I say, 'and Matthew. Surely you know me.'

'Know you?' Matthew frowns. 'Who are you?'

'Me,' I say. 'Myself.'

'Yourself?'

'Exactly,' I say. 'Returned,' I explain.

'But who?'

'Brother Diggory,' I say.

They consider this in silence. They look to each other. They frown.

'No, no,' says Huw, shaking his head. 'There was a Brother Diggory . . . but the Lord took him.'

'He died of the pestilence,' says Matthew, 'and he was

just a boy. Not a grown man like you.'

'Surely,' I say, 'you know my face? I used to help you with the horses,' I said. 'Clover, the skewbald mare, was always your favourite.'

He squints. 'What are you? Some ghoul?' He steps backwards, out of my reach. 'It's true there's some strong resemblance in the face . . .'

'No. It's me, Diggory,' I say. 'Truly.'

'Are you his wandering spirit? Can you find no rest?'

'No.' I reach out my hand. 'Feel me. I am warm. I am solid. I am Diggory. For I never died. Or, if I did, it was only briefly.'

'Now I can see the likeness. But . . . you're much taller . . . you have a beard.'

'I was a boy, but I grew. Now I'm a man.'

They shake their heads. They come forward and pat me on the arm, and touch my shoulder, and confirm my warm, solid form.

'Come . . .' They lead me down the path to the misericord.

'We must go see Brother Gregory,' says Huw, 'he's the Abbot now. Do not fear. He is strict but he is fair.'

There is much I want to know. 'Is there a new doctor, now Fulco is gone?'

'We do not have one. We are only nine brothers,' says Huw. 'We are building anew. These things take time.'

Brother Gregory shuffles forward. He eyes me from tufty head to grimy toe. He hears Huw tell the story. He takes me back with a scowl and a hug. He says I am the Prodigal Returned.

Close up, he smells of fusty apples and goat's cheese. Beneath the tips of his finger-nails are crescents of black dirt. Bristly clumps of white hair curl out of his ears. He is shorter than me now. His red nose is swollen and pitted like a strawberry. A small ball of snot hangs from a nostril, dangling on its stalk, straining to fall.

He starts to lecture me. He raises his voice for command and effect. He stabs the air with his fingers. Then he joins his hands, interlocking fingers, so they can wrestle each other and display his sincerity.

I do not follow every word of it all, for I am looking about me, seeing how things are changed for the worse. But some of his words pass through my mind.

He says I must straightaway shave my head, strip myself of my profane clothes, and dress in a tunic and cowl, to submit myself anew to the disciplines of our order.

He says I must do penance for leaving the brotherhood without seeking permission. He says I should crawl on all fours twice around the chapel. In the sight of all the other brothers.

He says he would then hear my confession, regarding my sordid time in the world. He warns I must tell all, however shocking, and hold nothing back.

I look on politely. I hold my tongue. I do not ask where he was when I was left here alone, burying our dead, saving Odo's treasures.

I do not challenge him by telling him that I am the true

Abbot – with the true Abbot's ring as proof, albeit stowed up my arse – and he just some late pretender. And I do not ask why, in God's name, I should fashion my habits and character on his sorry example.

I had returned to my home after a long time away. I had come in hope with good faith and a clean heart. I had come for a fond reunion. I had come to recommence my life as a monk.

But looking to Abbot Gregory and the few other brothers, and the ramshackle buildings, and neglected gardens, I realised the monastery was no longer the place for me.

It was empty of scholars now Fulco was gone.

There was nothing to learn here that I did not know already.

I sensed obedience had become too steep and narrow a path for me.

I had enough of cramping my hand copying copies of copies, with no freedoms, save for small scribbles in the margins.

My calloused hands confided they had dug enough gardens.

I enjoyed women. So chastity would no longer suit me.

I had fallen out of the habit of praying seven times a day.

I needed some further acquaintance with sin, before I sincerely resigned life's pleasures.

I'd grown used to having meat on my platter. With gravy.

And hair upon my scalp.

And my own thoughts in my head.

Between Vespers and Compline, the Abbot and I walked out to where the gardens had been. The land was heavily overgrown, fed, I suppose, by so many dead brothers, giving of themselves back to the world.

I guessed the places to dig from the lie of the land, pacing out the distance to the buildings, then correcting for the growth of my steps, between here and then.

Brother Huw dug. Brother Matthew held the torch, flickering and spitting in the drizzle.

This way they recovered much – coins in a cooking pot, silver altar furniture, bundles of manuscripts, parcelled in oiled cloth, reliquary boxes, only part rotted, vestments rolled up in leather sacks.

We went to the chapel to celebrate Compline, and God's great bounty, and the gifts returned to us from the dead.

As the brothers trod their way back to their cells for sleep, I let myself out of the monastery by the side gate and strode away into the night.

XXIII. I Find My Home and Helpmeet

Yew Wood is the village of my birth, nine long miles from the monastery. I had not been back there for a decade, since I was seven.

I thought I would recognise the houses, bridges and meadows, but nothing looked familiar. Everything was meaner, smaller and tighter than I had expected.

All that came back of my childhood there were brief snatches of summer-time. Getting stung on the tongue by a wasp as we shared an apple. Diving into the river and from the bottom seeing the dancing sun, between the reed stems, through a golden haze of cloudy water. Running through the barley field with my friend Maddy.

The main street was narrow and pitted, the houses in poor repair, as an incessant rain loosed the mud underfoot to a thin brown treacle.

I stopped a man and asked after my grandfather.

'Do you know where I can find Luke Fox?' I said.

'Old Luke Fox?' He whistled. 'Back there.' He pointed to the church, the way I had come. 'In the grave-yard.'

'Working there?' I asked, for Luke often cut the grass and trimmed the hedging.

'Sleeping the rest of the dead,' he said, and crossed himself.

I stopped some moments, and said a prayer, moist-eyed in remembrance.

When I wander into the Three Moons inn, the company promptly falls silent. All eyes turn on me.

I try to strike up a conversation with the landlord. I ask him for a jug of ale.

He answers, informing me that he has a sore tooth. He says it is the same sore tooth he has had these past two days. And nights.

He says it mars his mood. And then he invites me to commit an unnatural intimacy upon myself, sticking my parts where they cannot go, and never belong.

He remarks that he is a hospitable and kind-hearted man but, as things stand, he would as happily twist off my head with his bare hands as serve me any beer. So, I'd better move on.

'Which tooth?' I ask.

'Why?' he growls. 'Is that any business of yours?'

'I am a surgeon and apothecary.'

He scowls at me some moments, then sways my way, turning his head sideways. He slowly opens his gappy jaws and points to the weeping green stump and livid red gum at the side of his mouth.

'There,' he says.

'Shall I free you of it,' I say, 'and stop your pain?'

He grunts. Reluctant, he nods.

I say he must first chew on some henbane, which I fetch from my pouch of herbs, to soothe the pain, and that as

I travelled without tools, I shall need small blacksmith's tongs, nut-crackers, or two metal spoons. Else a small hammer and chisel.

But then the blacksmith, who is drinking in the tavern, says he has the very implement I need – some long-handled chainmail pliers.

The dozen drinkers in the tavern draw around to watch the show. They make some mockery of my youth and untidy appearance. A couple of small wagers are struck as to the success of my performance.

The offending tooth being a jagged, weeping stump, there is not much to hang on to, so leverage is in short supply. But I dig deep, into his swollen gum, and perse-vere with the pincers, as if my life depends on it, climbing onto my toes, while the landlord starts yelping a high-pitched whine, like a whipped puppy, and keeps stamping his foot, until I hear the creak, followed by the crack, that comes as the tooth finally yields its last tenure on his jaw. And it flies out, over the heads of the onlookers, landing with a clank in the fireplace.

The audience stamp their feet and bang their fists on the refectory table to show their approval.

'God's bones . . .' remarks the landlord. His spits a gob-ful of pale yellow pussy stuff, while a stream of blood arcs up and out from the side of his mouth.

He shakes his head, smiles and remarks, 'Sweet Jesus. I feel better for that.'

He lays a tankard of ale before me. He beams at me lopsided through swollen, blood-smeared lips. He pats my back. He calls me 'friend'. He asks me who I am and where I hail from.

I tell him I come from this very parish. That my mother was Mattilda Fox, and her father Luke Fox. I say I was given over to the monastery at Whye, where I trained as a scribe, surgeon and apothecary.

He says, 'Welcome home . . . son.' He says I must forgive the initial unfriendliness. But the company mistook me as some unnecessary stranger from some foreign place.

He remarks that I am to be welcomed too for my skills, since there is no doctor or surgeon thereabouts, or in any of the neighbouring parishes, for the plague had taken two, while the others have fled.

Then other drinkers declare they have teeth that I might pull for them.

And a swine-herd shows me his infected leg, which I bathe and bandage, and also his dog's mastitis, which I say he might cure with a poultice of cabbage leaves.

As the day passes, news spread around the village of the arrival of medicine.

So, I am much in demand and get called here and there, to puncture seven sheep that have the bloat from a surfeit of clover, de-horn a boisterous bull, lance some boils, treat some colic, medicate some canker, remedy some scouring in piglets, and bandage some weeping leg ulcers.

I attend upon many and various patients, animal and human, with conditions malignant and trivial.

Often I have full knowledge of what I am doing, and a

suitable treatment for their particular complaint. Many are grateful. Several feel better after. None die.

In return I am, for the very first time in my life, paid for my labour – receiving duck eggs, barley loaves, turnip tops, promises, a kiss, mugs of ale, and some pennies.

Franklin the landlord promises me free lodging for the night.

'Do you know what I think you should do, Jack?' He lays his heavy arm on my shoulder and tweaks my cheek.

'What's that?'

'I think you should stay at the inn here, and rent a barn from me, to treat the sick, and hire some garden space to grow your herbs.'

I say that sounds a promising prospect.

'You seem like a calm, agreeable, kindly man. Who likes to help people. And has a trade and many skills.'

'Thank you.'

'It would benefit us both. For I would give you a roof. And you would draw custom to my premises.'

Then he confides that there is one further good deed I can do for him, should I be willing, that would make him happy and content me too.

'Yes,' I say, 'what's that?'

'You could marry my daughter, Faith.'

'*Marry?*' I say. 'Your daughter?'

It comes as a sudden, surprising invitation.

I do not want to offend him, my new best friend. But I have to confess that I have no feelings for his daughter, having never met her.

'She is my only daughter. She is very precious to me. I am offering you a great gift.'

'Yes?' I enquire. 'What is she like?'

'She has a very strong mind,' he says, 'and is pleasantly plain to the eye.'

'Is that good, in a wife?' I ask. For you can be married till death do you part, and spend years regarding your spouse, full in the face.

'Never make the mistake I did . . .' He sighs, looking solemnly to the ground. 'If you marry a beautiful wife, you will have no peace or rest. There'll be no end to your troubles. The beautiful grow vain from watching their own reflections. They will drive you to distraction, always asking you to look at them, and remark upon their appearance, saying, "Is my hair better like this, or like that?" "Am I prettier than the milkmaid?" "Do I look younger than my daughter?" "Which is the lovelier, my right side or the left?" "Would you care to see the pimple on my arse?" "Is my muff too furry?" "Do my toes look plump?"'

'Yes?' I say. 'I did not know.'

'And honesty is no solution.'

'It isn't?'

'For other men will pay her compliments, when you forget to, and try to prey on her. As soon as they see you riding your horse for market, they will go knock on your door, with a thought to mounting her in your place.'

I consider all this in silence, trying to sift the sensical apart from the sly.

218

'So Faith is a fine choice. She is young, lively, healthy and strong-minded. She has broad hips for birthing children, strong arms for lifting, and a confident voice that carries far. She is a fine girl. She isn't marred by beauty. Yet she isn't ugly either. But you mustn't mind the shouting.'

'Shouting?' I ask.

'Nor the throwing, neither.'

'The *throwing*?' I say.

'It's nothing,' he reassures. 'She means little by it . . . But sometimes she throws things . . .'

'What things?'

He shrugs. He gestures vaguely, wafting the airs with his empty hands. 'Things close by. That come to hand. Things that travel well. Through the air.'

'Oh.'

'It is a habit. She breaks things . . . Or sets them alight. Or pours water on them. Rips them with a knife. Or crushes them with a hammer. Pulls them apart with her hands. Or calls them foul names.'

'Why so?' I enquire.

'It is her great sincerity. She has too big a heart. She's impetuous. She feels too strongly. There's no harm in her. Only too much feeling.'

'Those are great virtues,' I encourage him, 'big-heartedness and sincerity.'

'So, when she is happy, she is very happy. And when she is sad, she is very sad. And when she is angry, I leave the house.'

'I understand,' I say.

219

'So any man she loved would be very blessed, under the welter of her love.'

'I see,' I agree.

'But any man who crossed her would be very sorry.'

'Yes?'

'So, a man who treated her well would have nothing to fear.'

'Indeed.'

'So?' He leans forward and taps my shoulder. 'What do you think?'

'About what?'

'About wedding my daughter Faith.'

'Oh.' I grow evasive. 'I would certainly have to meet her first.'

'Good.' He taps my shoulder again. 'You may call me Father, if you wish.'

He was as good as his promise. So the next day he introduced me to the full of it. He showed me the barn, behind the inn, where I might treat the sick, the square of garden between the barn and the brew-house where I could grow my herbs, the nearby stream for clean running water, and Faith the daughter with the child-bearing hips, whose throwings and shoutings I should learn not to mind.

The tenor of his remarks was that this was a take-it-or-leave-it, all-or-nothing offer – requiring my acceptance of each and every condition, but to be sweetened by a dowry of seventeen shillings and three pence, a bedstead, two nanny goats, and a set of copper pans for cooking.

220

Of course, as a careful man, I took care to consider each clause, and turn over every item in my mind.

i. Yew Wood as a place to settle.

There were only two places on this Earth I could claim as home – the monastery at Whye, and here at Yew Wood. I was born here. I had a history. I was known of. I had a place in people's memory.

My grandfather's brother lived here, and two of his sons. I had family of sorts. I was welcome.

ii. The outbuilding, to be my infirmary.

The barn was more than satisfactory, being twenty paces by fifteen, with a sound roof and a dry stone floor, and a double door with a south-westerly aspect.

There was ample space for a table for operations, beds for the sick, racks for medicines, with the scope to partition an area off for times and occasions requiring some privacy, such as amputations, sleeping, or taking refreshments.

iii. The garden, to be my herbarium.

This was a plot directly behind the outhouse, currently lushly grassed. The soil was a fine, rich loam, damp but well drained. Within this was the spare ground I should need to dig out trenches to fill with other soils, which I discovered I could source nearby. For I should need a wet clay soil for the barberry, burdock, borage, comfrey and foxglove. I should need a drier, sandier soil for the rosemary, sage, basil, chervil, mint, oregano, parsley and thyme.

iv. The stream to supply clean water.

This water fell through a stony course from an underground river which broke to the surface twenty paces above. It was cool, clean-tasting, clear to the eye, and not open to farm animals to foul it.

v. Faith to be my helpmeet.

Faith proved the most difficult item to assess. I recognised the landlord's true account of her, with respect to both her character and comeliness. Yet I was cautioned by how others spoke of her. For she was known in the village as Fey Fay, and said by some to be moon-struck, crazy as a coot, and the village idiot.

But her father reminded me that marriage was a long and difficult journey, and an agreement to fight the world as a couple, back to back, to share property and raise children.

He warned me that beauty was only face-deep. It faded quickly, and passion soon fled. So that the best choice in a wife would be for a strong-armed, determined, big-boned fighter, to mind your back.

XXIV. The Secrets of Woman
and Her Dark Interior

I am becoming well known in all directions, in the villages hereabouts, for my skills as a surgeon and herbalist. I treat all who need my help – rich and poor, free and serf, young and old, man and woman, bull and cow, cock and hen, duck and drake, boar and sow, dog and bitch, stallion and mare, billy-goat and nanny.

And yet I always have my specialism, my favourite patients. For the Lord has directed my gaze to Adam's spare rib. So I have made myself expert in the maladies of the female of the humankind. And will always attend to her needs ahead of man or livestock.

Woman has always stood apart and unique as a mysterious organism, since the Day of Her Late Creation, and her body is a strange, concealed land, as yet only part revealed to the eyes of man and the scrutiny of science.

Whereas the male wears his sex candidly, openly on the outside, woman is devised as a puzzle, wrapped up in a mystery, concealing her sex within, in a labyrinth of tunnels. So while the testicles of the man hang outside in a handy purse, for all to see, alongside his utensil, the testicles of the woman are untouchable, carried deep inside, and are even known by a different name.

Truly, there is so much that man and woman share in their design, yet there's so much that divides them too.

Such that women develop maladies and distempers entirely their own. Prominent amongst these are –

   i. Starvation of semen, leading to chastity-fever.
  ii. Suffocation of the womb.
 iii. Wandering uterus.
 iv. Failure to conceive a son.

So this has become my calling as surgeon and apothecary. To bring reason, medicine and the light of observation to bear, upon the bodies of women. Thus I have become an explorer of the female realm, a doctor of the distaff.

To this end, I am writing a text for the instruction of all practitioners of medicine, to promote my growing reputation, being candidly titled – *The Secrets of Woman: Being the True Revelation of the Enigmas of Her Dark Interior.*

And, as a married man, I have the privilege to take the good counsel of my wife, Faith, to inform my understanding, straight from the horse's mouth, by filling some man-shaped holes in my knowledge. Such as – How many days in each moon do you bleed? Is it true, as Zeno observes, that menstruation attracts bears? Why do women squat to pass water, instead of standing like a man? And what, pray, is woman's reason for so favouring that pastime known as kissing?

But it is Doctor Galen who gives us best entry to women. For the opening to unlocking her mysteries lies in the four elements.

Elementally, man is hot and dry.

Whereas woman is wet and cool.

And from this fundamental difference, much else quickly follows.

The heat of the male converts some of his bloods to semen.

Yet woman, possessed of less heat, cannot effect this same conversion. Her blood forms itself to a lesser, weaker seed, and that left over leaks out in her menses. Or, if she is pregnant, if feeds the foetus in the womb, or is converted into milk if the child be born.

Woman has been designed by God to be cooler than man. This is not her fault nor any weakness, but just the Divine instruction the Lord gave to her body, the brief house of her soul.

While man is obedient to the fire of the sun, woman observes the cool, monthly cycle of the moon.

Woman is incomplete. She stands in regular need of the seed of man. She requires it for its liquidity, to wet her humours within.

If it is not forthcoming, she must demand it of her husband, that he give her his seed, and pleasure her well and often, with spasms of love, lest her equanimity be lost in a cold, dry chastity.

She may suffer the condition known as suffocation of the womb. Then, lacking the male moisture of semen, the uterus may wander about the body in search of another wetness elsewhere, so causing mischief to that woman's health by displacing her organs within. If this happens, the womb may still be lulled back to its proper position, if coaxed by sweet perfumes, placed outside the body, close to the vulva, so that the enticing scent may carry inwards and upwards. For the very same scents as pleasure a woman's nose likewise gratify her vagina.

To conceive, a woman must have regular monthly bleeds. So, if these menses are not forthcoming, they must be encouraged to return. The proper treatment is this –

Take a hot bath each day and, as she bathes, the woman should drink ale spiced with speedwell and centaury. After bathing, she must be covered warm while the doctor rubs her privates to coax the flow of blood to these parts, before applying a poultice to her vulva of barley meal, wild celery and mugwort. This to be repeated as many days as necessary.

But if, on the contrary, the menses are too heavy and vigorous, the reliable treatment is this –

Throw upon the hearth the fresh, moist droppings of a female horse. Have the woman stand close and raise her hem so that the smoke fills her skirt, draws the sweat from her legs, and finds its way upwards, drifting where it will.

When a woman lies with a man for intercourse, she releases her menses at the same time that the man releases his semen, so the male and the female seeds enter the womb together and are mixed, by the quiver and jerks of their gratified desires. Thus the woman conceives.

226

But only if she first be pleasured.

Praise be to God.

Then the womb closes up like a purse, so nothing can fall out. And after, the woman no longer menstruates.

When any woman says she wishes to conceive, I tell her this –

Your womb is hotter and drier on the right side. It is wetter and cooler on the left. So if you desire to conceive a boy, you should after intercourse lie on your right side so the seeds of procreation fall to that side. Or – should you prefer a girl – you should lie on the left.

Otherwise, let the husband collect the vagina and womb of a hare, dry them, powder them, and drink this sprinkled in wine. Then the woman will conceive a girl. But if she wants a boy, let her collect the testicles of the hare, desiccate and powder them. Then she will conceive a boy.

If a man and woman wish to conceive but are unable, you can determine whose fault this is by having each piss upon a separate bowl of bran meal. Whichever bowl of meal rots first discloses the faulty partner.

It is well known from the writings of Dame Trotula of Salerno that the embryo develops this way in the womb –

   i. First month – the male and female seeds join, mingling their blood.

  ii. Second month – the blood clots into a tiny body.

 iii. Third month – the nails and the hair develop.

iv. Fourth month – the foetus discovers motion and thereby makes the mother sick.

 v. Fifth month – the foetus develops the likeness of the father, or else of the mother.

vi. Sixth month – the baby grows a brain and nerves, so it may think and feel once born.

vii. Seventh month – the baby swells, growing solid and stronger.

viii. Eighth month – the infant is made whole and complete, blessed with all its parts.

 ix. Ninth month – the infant proceeds out of darkness into light.

But if a woman desires not to conceive, I can help her also. Then I advise her this way –

Carry against your naked flesh the womb of a goat which has never conceived. Then the sterility it imparts may pass from the flesh of the goat straight into you, absorbed through the skin.

Or, in another fashion, but to the same effect, I will advise –

Take a male weasel and let its testicles be cut away. But let the beast be released alive. Yet retain these testicles, and hold them to your bosom, having wrapped them tight in goose-skin. This way you will not conceive. For male potency has been cut off, and imprisoned in your power.

If a woman has given birth but chooses not to suckle the baby herself, she may prefer to hire a wet-nurse. Then, I advise her thus –

Whichever the sex of your own child, find a wet-nurse who has recently given birth to a boy. For the female body is wise in ways unknowing. It produces a milk for the boy that is richer and more nourishing than the milk for a girl. It is for this simple reason that boys grow bigger and stronger than girls.

So, a boy wet-nursed on girl's milk would likely grow up feeble and weakly.

Women often report that child-birth is painful, and evidence this well, with their howls and screams, attendant on the occasion. But this pain, the holy men say, is not without reason, being the reparation God requires of woman, so reminding her of the apple in Eden.

The Lord's Creation is immaculate, perfect. So it is God's Design, not any mistake, that every woman is required in every labour of birth to push a thing too large through an opening too small.

After a male child is born, there must be care where the umbilical cord is cut, for this decides the eventual length of the boy's organ.

If a man or woman finds themselves, through advancing years, with declining vigour to bring to the marriage bed, I recommend this cure to restore their pleasure in copulation –

Take five blind new-born puppies, by preference black and white, gut them, and cut off the feet, to allow their essence to flow out, then boil in water, and in this water have the patient rest for four hours after he has eaten, and whilst in the bath he should keep his head and chest completely covered with the fleece of a sheep, so he won't catch a sudden chill.

This is efficacious because a puppy contains the essence of growth, recovery and rebirth. For it is born lame but soon gets agile. It's born helpless yet quickly grows vigorous. It's born blind but then gains sight. And this recuperative essence, if not squandered on a dog, can be absorbed by the sickly soul, be they man or woman, of declining years.

Of course, there is still much else to be learned about the anatomy, ailments and feelings of women. But these are some of my discoveries, so far.

And I offer them up to you, in a spirit of generosity, as a gift of knowledge, the fruits of my research. For much of it isn't widely known yet.

XXV. Aristotle Misleads Me

Marriage can prove an awkward sacrament. At the start, the union of man and woman may fail to delight. Both parties may have to seek its perfection through practice, exercise patience, and cling to their faith.

You can find yourself an unhappy actor in this mummery of two players, sitting tongue-tied in the gloom, in silence long hours by the fireside, or lain in a bed, feigning sleep, in the resentful company of a stranger, of a contradictory sex, of uncertain temper, who seldom looks you in the eye, and maybe prefers to be somewhere else, and with whom you share little, save a confined space, and stale air, without any common cause, so intimacy is a dangerous leap in the dark, and you doubt the Almighty would ever want you joined so, till death do you part.

Yet there is always good in marriage too – not least in the acquisition of property, the dowry of livestock and household goods, and the new-found family you embrace and enjoin.

Then there remains the physical act – the love in God's garden – that the man and wife come to enjoy. He with his seed and dibber. And she with her secret pot.

I have let it be known to my wife, Faith, that she may take her full and lengthy pleasures of my body just as often as she cares to. And draw off as much seed as she needs.

My wife, Faith, in return, lets me know exactly how I should satisfy her, and directs me fully, each step of the way, in the varied dances of our desire, showing what goes where, at what pace we proceed, who is backwards, and who is forwards, topsy-turvy, on top, or bottom, and who should lead and who should follow, and who comes first, and who calls the tune, and who should pay the piper, and who can go fiddle.

Forgive the candour of my forthright rhetoric.

I do not say Faith is strict in the saddle. I rather say she is determined and ardent. But sometimes she rides me rough, then claws too deep and bites too hard. Or leads us off where nature never intended.

Perhaps I have told too much already. Pray, wipe it from your mind. And think no more about it. I would not have any dark imaginings thrust into your unsullied mind.

A surfeit of passion is surely less a fault than the lack of it. Only I have a thin skin and bleed easy.

I cannot exaggerate our great joys, now we have a son, Faith and I. We have christened him Francis Fulco Franklin Fox, after the Saint of Assisi, my tutor Brother Fulco, and his mother's father.

My darling Faith often remarks how closely he takes after me, both in his looks and his ways. Though, to most eyes, with his plump limbs, fat face, near-bald scalp, he most closely resembles any other baby.

And, as for his manners, when he is not suckling – for which he has great appetite and prodigious talent – he

232

sleeps. If he is not passing wind. When he is not crapping himself or pissing. Which he does more than you might think him capable, for such a small contraption with so few, small holes to let it all out.

His was a slow and difficult birth, and he arrived early, seven months after our marriage and first consummation, although well developed and of a larger than usual size.

This is a condition known to medicine as a precocious birth, consequent on accelerated incubation, when the father has galloping semen of exceptional speed and vigour. So hastening the course of the pregnancy.

I would say Francis is a perfect child.

Though some observe that he has a large nose and prominent ears that face to the front. But I would reply he is designed that way for a purpose. The Lord's purpose. For he is God's Own Creation, and shaped just the ways the Almighty intended.

Oh, woe.

I am reluctant to engage you any further in my sorrows.

But there's one final tragedy I have to report.

It was James Langtree, the new vicar of Saint Alban's, a man of some inexperience, being barely older than me, who first alerted me to the well-being of my dearest wife and helpmeet, Faith.

He strolled up to me outside the inn. He wished me good-day. Then he asked me, with a look of some profound concern, if my wife was unwell.

'Faith?' I said. 'She is in vigorous good health. I am a

233

surgeon. I am expert in the maladies of women. I live with her. I lie with her. We talk almost every day. And, once a week, I taste her waters. If she were unwell, I would surely know it.'

'It's just I saw her a short time back . . .'

'Yes?'

'She was eating in the grave-yard.'

'Eating?'

'Grass . . .'

'Grass?' I enquired, lest I'd misheard.

'And dock leaves.'

'Dock leaves?'

'And nettles.'

I creased my brow. I thought awhile. Then I spoke carefully, describing things simply, for a stranger to medicine. 'The body is wise,' I explained, 'sometimes it craves what it lacks. But without knowing why. Dock leaves are a known medicament. And nettles are a proven acidic, that can offset a surfeit of bile.'

'It's just she was on all fours,' the pastor went on, 'grazing.'

'Grazing, you say?'

'Like a cow.'

'Cow?'

'When I spoke to her, she looked back at me in silence. Then she rolled her big, brown eyes. She was working her jaws from side to side, as if she was chewing the cud.'

'Now, that,' I exclaimed, 'is unusual for Faith. And not in her true character. You can be sure I shall look into it.'

'It would be best,' the pastor agreed. 'There may be some damage done to her mind. Or some malignant possession . . .'

'Possession?'

'Luke, chapter eight, verse two,' he said. '"Certain women had been healed of evil spirits . . . Mary called Magdalene, out of whom went seven devils".'

'My wife is not possessed of anyone – save herself. She is a strong-willed woman,' I explained, 'she is known for it. She has always held her own opinions, and gone her own peculiar ways . . .'

We wished each other good-day. But he'd set me thinking, and encouraged me to observe my wife with a refreshed interest.

To be sure, it was not just grass and dock leaves. Once I'd started watching, I found that Faith had taken to consuming all manner of stuff folk do not normally enjoy eating, or have the juices to digest – leather, twigs, rose-buds, pieces of parchment, duck feathers, cloth, chalk, charcoal, or pieces of mortar she'd scratched out of the wall.

She seemed insatiable, as if she must always have some unnatural matter in her mouth to chew over. The compulsion went so far as to quell her conversation. Hers was a condition of unnatural appetites, well known to science as *sensualitis contra naturam*.

I cannot say Faith made a quick recovery. Rather, she seemed to slide into a slow decline.

Soon, she had developed further foibles. She started

235

smelling things that were not there. And hearing things that hadn't sounded.

'Have you spilled some vinegar?' she'd say, sitting up in bed.

'Why are they ringing the church bells,' she'd demand, 'in the middle of the night?'

'What is burning?' she'd ask. 'Is it the bread?'

'Who is that laughing, under the bed?' And she demanded I get down on my knees to look beneath.

'I think the cat has shat itself, Jack,' she'd remark, sniffing the air. 'You'd best go clean up the mess.'

She would have been graced, had she been gifted some beautiful scents – perfumes, incense, rare aromatics, and floral blooms – and heard fine choral music. But mostly she detected loud noise, and sour, acrid stench.

I gained a further concern. I began to worry if she was fit to take good care of our child, Francis. For I found she had taken to feeding him on boiled twigs, and washing him seven times a day, scouring his skin raw, to try to stop the smell he did not have. That only she imagined.

Despite suffering this disorder, still she was blessed in another way, in compensation – being married to a man of medicine, who could decipher her illness and deliver sound treatments as remedy.

For, by now, I had deduced the cause of the infirmity.

I knew that Faith must have some malign growth in her head, some worm or canker in her brain, that was eating up her capacities. First it had taken many of her inhibitions. And some of the respect due to her husband. Then her sense of taste, and now her aptitudes for smell and hearing. Her brain was eating itself. Each day I saw her diminished, emptied a little more. Every time she woke, there was less of the Faith I married, and more of a void, in that vacant, silent, slack-eyed shell.

So I knew I must find some curative treatments, before she was quite lost to us.

It is difficult for medicine to reach through to the brain. It's an inaccessible organ, imprisoned in that rock-hard cage we call the skull.

So the best resource we have is to trepan.

You must choose the exact spot on the scalp and saw out a circular hole in the bone below, so exposing the brain, throbbing grey, with a map of pink veins, beneath the thin cover of two membranes.

Then you must take a silver spoon and scoop out the sick tissue, taking no more than you need to. Finally you must seal the hole in the skull by slotting a coin into the gap, and tapping it tight with a wooden mallet.

It may sound simple enough. But it leaves a bald, metallic scar that will never heal. And there are risks – of a bleed on the brain, or a fester to the wound, or some unintended damage to the patient's capacities.

For the mind is a delicate organ. And much of it has a use. So you cannot just spoon it out, willy-nilly.

But we must do what we are able to. We cannot just sit on our hands. We must try what we can.

*

I wish I could say the first attempt was a triumph, but it transpired that Faith had a badly organised mind, with its functions scrambled, laid in all the wrong places. At least not where Doctor Aristotle had advised I should find them. Her reason was lodged where her smell should be, and her balance where her taste should reside, and her self-control was gone into hiding.

So the first operation just ended in a loss of her steadiness, causing her to keep tumbling from the upright, without any due reason, but did nothing to return her to her full senses.

Then the second operation made no discernible difference. For her malady had progressed very fast in the meantime. So she promptly fell into a deep sleep for three days, before she perished without giving us reason or warning.

So, despite pledging all my skills to the task, and the finest crafts of medicine, and the wisdoms of Galen and Aristotle, I was, in the end, unable to save her.

We are but feathers on the breath of God.

XXVI. Fox's Law

Though I've had the good fortune to marry two good women, so far, the first of great beauty, and the second of conspicuous character, these unions have been blighted by brevity. For my first marriage lasted only three days, and my second only eighteen months. My mother and I were together in this world for no more than a blink of the eye before she passed on, and, being just born, I was too young and unworldly to take her in. So the women in my life have come and gone in such blurry haste that I cannot claim to have come to know any of them well.

And every day I think of my dear departed wife, Faith, and thank God for all the good she did me. For, while she was harsh with her hands and wild with her tongue, and fierce with her throwings, still she did so much to establish me in life. For she helped me set myself up as a doctor, and provided me with my home, and gave me my precious son.

She may yet help me to a happier future, and longer marriage, perhaps with her friend, the Widow Caroline. For I have cast my eye her way. And, if the widow winks a blue eye, and proves willing, the rest of me might promptly follow.

Not all the news is dismal.

The plague is more or less defeated.

Yet at a terrible cost. Nearly half the folk of this nation are lost. So many high and mighty people were taken, replaced by no more than their offspring. Even the bishops and barons look like children these days.

You must imagine our people as a book with half the words missing. We do not make sense any more. Much of our story is lost, rubbed out. We do not link or join together as we did. Our sense of connection is lost.

We are so reduced in number, those who are left know their true worth. For there are not enough of us now. Doctors, priests, princes, labourers, husbands, wives, sons and daughters are all in short supply.

There are still outbreaks of plague, here and there, now and then. But it does not spread like wild-fire, the way it did before. Nowadays, it mostly claims babes and toddlers, the very young.

Perhaps it is God's will. Perhaps He does not require those who suffered the plague before to suffer it once again.

Or perhaps we have gained some defence, and carry some feeling in our hearts, knowledge in our minds, or belief in our bloods that protects us.

Perhaps medicine has won the day.

Now I am come eighteen years of age, and I am not without experience.

I have lived apace, having been born, died, raised to Heaven then resurrected.

But nothing happens for nothing. I believe I've been marked out as special. And several times saved from early death by Our Lord's intervention. I believe the Lord has some special use for me which the future will shortly reveal.

I know what to do. I must give my time and cleverness to the pursuit of truth. Through science. To play my part, helping folk to secure the sure cure for the pox, and for all manner of maladies, unveil the full mysteries of God's Design of Man and Woman, and discover the truths all-chemical, revealing the Philosopher's Stone, the Elixir of Life, so we may convert dross into gold, and so give wealth to the world.

The Almighty has made our minds brilliant, that we may understand the laws of His dominion, the physics of the heavens, and the beauty of His Creation.

We know so much already. In a few generations, we may come to know it all.

Now my studies are concerned with the computations of the flesh, examining the additions and subtractions involved in the world, and particularly those transactions of the body, concerning ourselves, both by taking the outside in, and giving back to the world, turning our insides out.

I have designed a series of weighing-scales which enable me to balance myself, and my smaller bodily incomes and expenditures, against a series of metal bars, ranging from large to some so tiny they are thin as a hair.

By this methodology, a scholar is able to weigh himself, throughout each day, and all that enters his body, as food and drink, and whatever leaves it, by whatever route, including the smallest amounts of this. And that. Even the other. So far as including the dribbles of mucus that flee his nose, the clippings of his finger- and toe-nails, the stubble he shaves daily from his face, and the waxy smears that depart his ears. Which group together, in the language of higher science, by the term 'returns' or 'outgoings', to be offset against 'incomings'.

Outgoings	Incomings
Shit	Food
Piss	Drink
Snot	Ointments
Squirts, leaks and sundry juices	Powders and potions
Hair, nails et alia	Divers herbs
The soul (at death)	The soul (at conception)
3 parts by weight	8 parts by weight

And from this calculation I have made the profound discovery – to be known to the world of scholarship as Fox's Law – that, for every eight poundage a person puts in his body, only three poundage ever comes out. Yet a person stays much the same weight.

It is this perplexing, miraculous loss that leads me to describe the human body as a dematerialising engine, for its mysterious and ingenious capacity to continuously turn something solid into less than nothing.

And yet, I know that the missing matter must be passing somewhere, somehow.

I have divined that this freight of weighty matter passes invisibly in the airs, through the bodily processes of expiration and oration, perspiration, respiration, expectoration, lubrication, vibration, relocation, excitation, suppuration, and transpiration, where its smell can still be detected, and its dampness still felt in the air.

It is this that leads me to call the atmosphere that surrounds us solid air or immanent matter, meaning that, though transparent, it is full of stuff, that can suddenly manifest, passing back from the unseen state to the seen, and from the airy to the solid form through spontaneous re-materialisation, or precipitations, including the sudden appearance of new things never seen by man before, as well as the more common effects known as fog, clouds, rain, hail, drizzle, snow, and the downpour of small beasts, most commonly newts, frogs, and small fishes, such as frequently happens in Flanders.

It is the sudden heavy traffic of matter through the air that causes the phenomenon of wind, bending the trees, tugging the hats from men's heads, and pushing all things from its path, seen in extreme forms as hurricanes and storms, battering down houses, even, with the sheer force of weighty invisibilities.

Likewise, it is the normal downward weight of this heavy saturated air, known as gravid-ity, pressing down upon us from above, that holds us trapped to the ground. Which, though a weighty burden upon us all, is not without its benefits. For though it holds us earth-bound, it gives us discipline and tenure upon *terra firma*, and prevents us from drifting up and away.

Whereas Brother Fulco concerned himself with the all-chemy of matter, turning base stuff into precious, I have found an issue yet more profound. For I am engaged with the all-chemy of life, by which dead, inert matter can be converted to the living.

It is my quest to find the spark of life, and ignite dead matter into living, breathing stuff.

To this end, I have been busy making a small being, a homunculus, or tiny man. For I came upon an arcane procedure in the text *Secretum Secretorum* – *The Secret of Secrets* –

Let the sperm of a man be putrefied in a closed jar, then after sealed with horse dung for forty days in a horse's womb. Then it will take the semblance of a tiny man, yet transparent, without a solid body. But if you then incubate it for forty weeks in a kettle, feeding it daily with fresh man's blood, it will become a true and living infant. But tiny. Yet without a soul to call its own.

I worry for my darling son Francis when I am called away to travel and learn, and perhaps become celebrated amongst the scholars of the world. The sorry child already lacks a mother. Then, when fate or fame summons me away, the poor, pitiful orphan will lack a father too.

And because I am away from our home too often already, travelling to care for the sick, I have entrusted Francis's daily care to his mother's father, Franklin.

I intend for my son to have all the good fortunes I enjoyed. I want him to gain an education – to master Reading, Writing, Latin, French, Mathematics, Rhetoric, the Sciences, and grow up a man of conscience, and good character, in the fear of God, as a protector of children, and defender of women, dedicated to the welfare of all.

So, when he comes of age, reaching seven, I will take him to the brothers of the Order of Odo, at the monastery of Whye, to become an oblate, a gift to the Church. So he may enjoy all the bounties I have received. For his own benefit and the Lord's. That he may also learn charity, chastity, obedience, truth and faith, then proceed in my fortunate footsteps.

Perhaps he will follow me into medicine, one day knowing more than I. For each generation sees further and clearer than the one before, as we progress towards the fullness of knowledge.

For my part, I will continue as I have begun, as a student of nature and doctor of souls.

Discovering the Almighty's laws.

Healing with herbs, saw or knife.

Curing the sick.

Mending women.

God willing.

But now I must go attend my new offspring, my three homunculi, those little see-through men, dancing their jigs, their heads jerking wildly, their tiny pin eyes watching me with wonder, as they simmer in their three separate kettles, in the different stages of their incubation.

They emit a chorus of screechy, whistly sounds, like crayfish boiling in water.

I have named them Thomas, Richard and Harold.

Tom will reach full-term in ten days. Dick and Harry, the twins, are due their birth a week after.

To feed them the daily blood they require, I must go bleed myself, from the largest artery in my arm, collecting the most vital fluid I can spare before I fall faint.

I thank God that every last thing in His dominion has an exact pattern, knows His reason and works to His exquisite plan.

I think myself a fortunate man.

For, it is sure as fleas, if I had not been conceived out of trickery, through a mean-spirited monk on the Pope's errand, orphaned at birth, given away to a monastery, educated as scholar and doctor, taught the truths of Saint Odo, killed by the pox, been spoken to by Death himself, given a sight of Hell, then raised to Heaven, told the meaning of life by the Almighty radiance which is Our Lord, and been then resurrected to the rude clamour of life, befriended a rat, been robbed in the woods by a one-legged man, led to discover woman, sentenced to death at the stake for debating philosophy in Latin with a pig, lived on to lick a salty leper, gone feral in the forest, been rescued by an epiphany of toads, become married to Faith, become father to Francis, and widowed a second time, when Aristotle misled me, I would not be here, now, with the cheery, silky-skinned, golden-haired, azure-eyed, rosy-cheeked Widow Caroline, with her scents of buttermilk and honey, who sees to all my domestic needs, in return for her board and three pennies a day, playing footsie before the warmth of this fire, peeling roasted chestnuts, sipping spiced mead, and wrestling my new Hurdy Gurdy, thinking of our imminent bed-time.

And may the great blessings of God shower down on you too.

also by Christopher Wilson

THE ZOO

Read on for the first chapter

faber

1. Over my head in history

My class teacher, Comrade Professor Mikhail Mikhailov, says in Amerika they have one hundred and seventy-three flavours of ice-cream and three hundred and seventy-six different models of motor car. While, here, in the Union of Socialist Republics we have five types of motor car. All black. And ice-cream is ice-cream flavoured, or chocolate.

All the same, in Kapitalist USA they despise other peoples, especially the black man, and their movies are always about being richer than your neighbours, kissing showgirls and killing foreigners. Even the comedies. While here in the Motherland, we have Comradeship, Justice-For-All, Freedom-in-One-Country, and the other fine thing. The one that begins with an 's' and ends with an 'ism'. Besides the whatsit that ends with an 'ology'. Even for the Chechens and Azerbaijanis. And sometimes Gypsies. For Jews too. So I know which is the place for money to prosper, and which is the better place for people.

Call me Yuri. Though I get called lots of names, such as *Yuri nine-fingers*, *Yuri the Confessor*, or *Yuri the Deathless*. But my full, formal title is Yuri Romanovich Zipit.

I am twelve-and-a-half years old and I live in the staff

251

apartments, in The Kapital Zoo, facing the sea-lions' pool, behind the bisons' paddock, next to the elephant enclosure, and I like to play the piano but I am no Sergei Rachmaninov because my right arm is crooked and stiff, so I mostly play one-handed pieces, such as are written for the army of one-armed veterans, who sacrificed a limb for the Motherland, fighting in the Great Patriotic War.

I am in the Junior Pioneers Under-Thirteens Football Team, but I am no Lev Yashin. Mostly, I play fourth reserve, because of my limping legs, which stop me running, so I get to carry the water bottles. I am good at biology but I am no Ivan Pavlov.

I am damaged. But only in my body. And mind. Not in my spirit, which is strong and unbroken.

When I was six-and-one-quarter years old I cross paths with worst luck. A milk truck smacks me from behind while I am crossing Yermilova Street. It sends me tumbling somersaults through the air before bringing me down to earth, head first on the cobbles. Then a tram comes along, and runs me over, behind my back.

Things like this leave a lasting impression.

But Papa always encourages me to make the most of my misfortunities. He says 'Every wall has a door' and 'What doesn't kill you makes you stronger.'

And whenever you complain to him, about anything – like injustice, weevils in porridge, getting punched on the nose at school, a broken leg, or losing fifty kopecks – he says, 'Well, count yourself lucky. There are worse things in life.'

As it turns out, he's three-quarters right. In time, all the bits of my head joined back together. Open wounds healed. Bones set. My legs mended, most parts. But there are some breaks in my brain, mostly in my thinking-departments, and without any clear memories of whatever came before.

I have some holes in my memory still. Sometimes I choose the wrong words. Or I can't find the right one, and lay my hands on the real meanings. Facts fly out of my windows. My feelings can curdle like sour milk. Sense gets knotted. Then it's hard to untangle my knowledge. I don't concentrate easily.

Other times I cry for no good reason. Except I am throbbing with sadness. Sometimes, I go dizzy and fall over. Then there are flashes of brilliant light – orange, gold and purple – and odd, nasty smells – like singed hair, pickled herring, carbolic, armpits and rotting lemons. Then I lose consciousness. They tell me I thrash about on the ground. And dribble frothy saliva. And ooze yellow snot through my nose. This is when I am having a fit. Afterwards I can't remember any of it. But I have new bruises, which is a good thing, because it is my body's way to remember for me what my brain has for-gotten. Maybe I need to change my trousers, as a matter of urgency.

So I am sometimes slow and forgetful. Except in recre-ations and games – like battleships, hang-the-Fascist, chess and draughts – where I excel, because then every-thing I need to know lies seen, and open, there in front of me. So I can just play the game, without having to remember what happened on Thursday morning, how many sides on a dodecahedron, how to spell *coccyx*, or the Kapital of Uzbekistan.

So, overall, Papa tells me, the fool in me is finely balanced by my cleverness. And he calls me a *pochemuchka*. A child who asks too many questions. Without a brake on his mouth.

Plus I have another problem. It's the unfortunate look of my face.

People keep staring at it. My face. And then start seeing things. That just aren't there.

They gaze at me. They stare like an animal caught in headlights. Then they break into a smile. Then I smile back. Before you know it we're talking. And, by then, we're lost. It's too late.

Papa says folk can't help it. They see sympathy in my features. They find kindness in my eyes. They read friendliness in the split of my smiling mouth.

Guess what? They think I care about them. Even though they're total, absolute, hundred-per-cent strangers. They think they know me. From somewhere. But they can't remember where.

Papa says my appearance is a fraud and a bare-faced liar. He says that – although I am a good child in many ways, and kind enough – I am not half as good as my face pretends.

Papa says my face is one of those quirks of inheritance, when two ordinary parents can mix to produce something

254

extreme and striking. You see it too with moths, orchids and axolotls.

He says my face is my very best, prize-winning quality. He says my smile is easy and wide. My features are neat and regular. My gaze is direct but gentle. It lends me a sweet and tender face. The very kindest face you'd hope to find. A face that seems to love whoever it looks upon.

Papa says it is a face that could have been painted by the Italian artist Sandro Botticelli, to show an angel on his best behaviour, sucking up to God.

It gives me grief, my sympathetic, wide-open, smiling face. Papa says I have a true genius for needless and reckless involvement in the private affairs of other people.

Also he observes I am foolhardy.

Beyond idiocy.

And that I talk without first thinking.

'Shhh . . .' he always says. 'Idiot child.'

He says that when my head hit the cobbles of Yermilova Street, every fragment of fear got shaken out. Now my Frontal Lobes are empty, he says. My common sense went next. Closely followed by my tact, and then my inhibitions.

Of course, there's a name for my condition. I suffer from *impulsivity* brought on by *cerebral trauma*. Which is a way of saying I talk a lot, and move a lot, and ask a lot of questions, and make up my mind quickly, and do things on the spur of the moment, and find new solutions to things, and say rude things without thinking, and interrupt people to tell them when they've got things wrong, and blurt things out, and change my mind, and make

255

strange animal noises, and show lots of feelings, and get impatient, and act unexpectedly. All of which makes me like other people. But more so.

Because I make friends easily. With people and with animals. I enjoy talking. To anyone, more or less. And meeting new animals. Especially new species who I have never had the fortune to converse with before.

I like to help. Even strangers. After all, we are all chums and Comrades, put in this life to help each other, and rub along together.

In particular, I provoke whatever you call it when *people-tell-you-too-much-about-themselves, even-though-it-is-secret-and-shameful, concerning-things-that-you-never-wanted-or-expected-to-hear, and-are-probably-best-kept-secret, unspoken, for-all-concerned*.

Like a *confidence*, but even worse.

A magnet attracts iron-filings. I attract confessions. Strongly. From all directions.

I only have to show my face in public and total strangers form an orderly line, like a kvass queue, to spill their secrets into my ears.

Soon, their honesties turn ugly.

'I am a useless drunk.' One says.

Or 'I cheat on my wife, on Thursday afternoons, with Ludmilla, with the squint, from the paint depot, whose breasts smell of turpentine. By chance, she's my brother's wife . . .'

Or 'I killed Igor Villodin. I hacked off his head with a spade . . .'

Or 'It was me who stole the postage stamps from the safe in the bicycle-factory office . . .'

Often they flush with shame. Sometimes they start sobbing. They pull terrible gurning faces or gesture wildly with their hands.

Then I have to say, 'I am sorry . . . but you are confusing me with my face. It's much kinder than me, but it's not to be trusted . . . Of course, I like you . . . But I cannot take on everyone's problems. Not all the time. I have a young life of my own to live.'

'Anyway,' I say, 'don't worry. Things are never so bad as you imagine. Everything considered . . . What is done is done. What doesn't kill you makes you stronger. Every wall has a door. Make the most of your misfortunities. They make you what you are in life, and different from all other people. This is the only life you get. You must pick yourself up and move on.'

Aunt Natascha says everyone wants to confess in life, like Raskolnikov in *Crime and Punishment*, because they need to be understood and find forgiveness somewhere.

And since Lenin did away with God, Praise the Lord, may he rest in peace, they must look elsewhere, and closer to home.

So, they pick on me.

And I encourage confidences, she says, because I am friendly, and my face tells them I possess a gentle kindness that can forgive them anything.

It's then that she tells me that she despises Uncle Ivan, because he is a pervert, of the sickest sort, always trying to kiss her, and putting his hand up her skirt, to touch her thingammy, demanding rumpty-tumpty, day and night, any room in the house, and so she wishes he were dead.

But if you ask me to choose my favourite meal, I would say Polish pork sausage with buttered cabbage and potatoes fried in goose fat. I admit it. Topped with braised onions on the side. I should be so lucky. With wild mushrooms in sour cream dressing. And for dessert I would have blueberries with ice-cream. In my dreams.

By choice, I would drink birch juice or cherry nectar each and every mealtime. My favourite colour is scarlet. Because it is the colour of excitement, Saturday, Revolution, our flag, and Dynamo Kapital football shirts. My favourite player is The Black Spider, goalkeeper Lev Ivanovich Yashin. My name day is November 18th. My special hobby is studying wild animals. I am a member of the Young Biologist Club of The Kapital Zoo. My favourite zoo animal is the Brown Bear (*Ursus arctos*) and my favourite rodent is Severtzov's Birch Mouse (*Sicista severtzovi*).

My Papa is Doctor Roman Alexandrovich Zipit – Professor of Veterinary Science – who specialises in Cordate Neurology, which is the study of whatever goes wrong inside the brains of animals, so long as they have a backbone, especially in The Kapital Zoo.

You've maybe heard of him. Most likely you'll have seen his photograph in *The Progressive Journal of Socialist Neurology*. He is well regarded around The Kapital, in the mental community and sick-animal circles. His writings are well known to almost everyone who closely attends the brains of elephants.

And because he is a world famous, respected veterinarian he gets to treat world famous animals including Count Igor, the Juggling Tiger in the State Circus, Golden Glinka the racehorse and Comrade Composer Shostakovich's Fox Terrier Tomka.

But I never brag about being the son of a famous man, because bragging comes before a fall. And Papa's nothing special. Not to look at. Not from the outside. Not so you'd notice. So you would have to unscrew his head and shine a torch into the depths of his fantastic, huge brain to see what is peculiar about him. And if you met him on the street you wouldn't think twice, except to admire his overcoat with the astrakhan collar. Besides he's bald with a limp and a stoop, and carries a musty scent along with a tarry taint of pipe tobacco.

The things I am going to tell you are all true. Absolutely, completely, totally true.

Almost.

Except for the small things I change. Because I have to.

But only events, times, names and places.

Because these are very complicated and most confidential affairs, and shady events, leading to dark happenings.

These are secrets hiding away in history.

I am trusting to your silence. Also, I have to protect you.

For your own safety.

So, shhh.

It would harm you to speak of any of this. Because you shouldn't know it. Not any of it. So best keep quiet as a mouse. And blind as a mole.

Even now, I don't understand everything. To grasp it all you would need to speak Georgian like a native, tell dirty jokes like a Mingrelian secret policeman, have a reindeer-horn pocket knife, with one of those special can-opener attachments, be able to drink two bottles of pepper vodka and still stay sober, be a consultant in Neurology, and a senior member of the Politburo, with a doctorate in assassinations.

Things are hidden within other things, like a nest of wooden dolls. There's murder, medicine, theatre, cookery, juggling, skulduggery, impersonation, elephants, fate, within a whodunit, inside a mystery, wrapped in a tissue of lies, stuffed in a cardboard box, locked up in the understairs cupboard.

The events I write about began in 1953, one year ago, in Karasovo, near The Kapital, when Papa and I get dragged off in the middle of the night to visit some very important people.

More than important, I'd say.

No lie.

Particularly Scarface Joe, Felix the Juggler, Alexei the Actor, Lev, Georgy, Nikita, Nicolai, Matryona the Maid, and shit-face-Erik.

But don't be fooled too easily. These are not their

actual, factual names. It is dangerous to speak their full, real names. Ditto, real places. And other stuff.

Trust me.

There are several titles and personages I cannot even mention – like the Gardener of Human Happiness, Engineer of Human Souls, First Secretary, Deputy Prime Minister, Duty Officer, Marshal of the Slavic Union, Pavel the Gatekeeper, and whatsisname.

But spending time with the un-nameable, top-rank people you quickly get sucked deep into shit, in the sewer of politics. Forgive my Bulgarian. Before you know it, you are sunk up to your neck in trouble. Then you are over your head in history.

So let me share the advice Papa gives me –

Don't slouch. Don't smile at strangers. People misunderstand. These are grave times. Be warned. Blow your nose, you're dribbling. Pay close attention. Stop gibbering like a demented gibbon. Mind your manners. Stay on your guard. Try not to scuff your shoes when you walk. Brush your teeth, morning and evening. Get an early night when you can. Keep your head down. Change your underpants. Don't confide in strangers. Shut the door, for pity's sake. Keep your lips sealed. If people ask you awkward questions, act simpleminded. Go to the lavatory when you can. You don't know when the chance will come again. Don't prattle on like a total idiot. Above all, don't mention politics, or voice opinions off the top of your head.

Papa says the song of our time is silence, and the moral is 'Shhh.'

It's best not even to state the obvious, or hint at what everyone knows.

We are living in an age that hugs silence and befriends the mute.

Our National Anthem has become a breathless hush.

He says, if you have to open your mouth, you should make sure that whatever you say is as bald and plain as a boiled noodle, and has been first approved by a Central Committee, published in *The Daily Truth*, or incorporated into a Five Year Plan. All praise to Comrade Iron-Man, Man of Steel, Kind Uncle, and Father of Our Nation.

Above all, you mustn't make jokes.

Especially not this one –

Question: What has a thousand legs and eats potatoes?
Answer: A Kapital meat queue.

Because that was the very pleasantry that gets Gennády Sharikov sent to the work camps for eleven years. So it's not worth telling it. Not in the long run. Just to pass the time with a stranger on a tram, who then smirks, then arrests you. Because you never know who you're talking to. It may be a plain-clothes Colonel in the People's Commissariat for Internal Affairs. And even walls have ears. Besides hunger is never funny. And it is malicious to laugh at other people's misfortunes and you-know-whats.

All that happened was very *dialectical*, which is not a foreigner's way of talking but actually a meeting of opposing forces, like two stags butting heads for one doe. So something has to give. And things can never be the same again. Papa says that is how history works, particularly Slav history, where things can just go from bad to worse, and from worse to awful, in the blink of an eye, and it's hard to get a good night's sleep, and enough to eat, and snow-proof felt boots, although the excitement, cold feet and hunger can provoke great Socialist music and heroic literature, and Social Realist painting, by way of compensations. All praise to the Party. All homage to Comrade Iron-Man.

As it happens, I love finding new words like *dialectical*, *epicentral*, *duodenum*, *catawampus*, *egregious*, *skulduggery*, *infinitesimal*, and then working them like crazy, maybe for a whole week or so, until they've lost all their shine and gone all *lackadaisical* and *lacklustre*.

But, trust me, everything that follows is as true, inedible and indelible as the scarlet birthmark on my right buttock, which Papa says looks the spit of a young Comrade Lenin in profile, facing leftwards.